What they have said about the

SHORT STORIES

of Daniel Hoyt Daniels

I loved your stories -- they are delightful, especially the surprise endings. They are even better than O Henry and Maupaussant. I read all thirty of them in two days; I couldn't stop myself.
> -- Maria Atansov, Hilton Head, SC

Well done.
> -- Jack Harris, Sarasota, FL

Poignant; touched my heart.
> -- Suzanne Brailey, Gloucester, MA

Extremely creative.
> -- Evelyn Harris, Lincoln, MA

Your tongue in cheek is indeed producing chuckles here. A great job.
> -- Capt. Giles Kelly, USNR, Ret, Washington, DC

Your stories delight me. Your characters are so funny.
> -- Suzy Wolf, Beaufort, SC

We liked your stories.
> -- Ed Wendell, Orange, VA

They all simply flow so beautifully.
> -- Nancy Parten, Monroe, NY

As though he were in the room, telling the story.
> -- Anne Harris, Sarasota, FL

We loved "Happy Thanksgiving" greatly. We were both very moved. You are a really great writer; I mean that. I shall Xerox it and send it to my children. This story is marvelous.
> -- Frances Huxley, Playwright, Concord, MA

What they have said about the
SHORT STORIES
of   Daniel Hoyt Daniels

I liked the prose style – easy to read, and the plots evolved smoothly. The use of words was carefully chosen and concise. The variety made each one stand out by itself. I especially enjoyed reading Baked Alaska, You Took the Words, My Brother-in-Law Is a Jerk, and A Few More Days. Each touched me in a different way.   Marie in A Few More Days is a wonderful character.   On finishing each of these stories, I had a warm feeling.

Your bitterness in the war stories did not surprise me. The tragic ending of each of them made me think and feel the pain of the protagonists. They were extremely well written.
>   -- The Hon. Irving Tragen, former US Ambassador Panama,
La Jolla, CA

Quite a few chuckles. You write very well and get the reader's attention right away, and your endings are wonderful. You are also able to write from a woman's point of view, like in "A New Start." "The Rabbit" is great! Reminds me of my time in South Carolina when I volunteered in a school there. I really enjoyed reading these stories.
>   -- Ingrid Lander, Longmont, CO

Interesting.
>   -- Buzz Richards, Falmouth, MA

Your book is delightful. We especially liked "Happy Thanksgiving" and "John Harvard Fantoma." "Bastille Day" has everything: nostalgia, youth, politics, sex, humor, and history.
>   -- Miriam Mauzerall, Dobbs Ferry, NY

My guests liked it too.
>   -- Tinica Mather, Silver Spring, MD

I like your style.
>   -- Nancy Myers, Beaufort, SC

I am savoring your stories   I chuckle to myself every time I think of "My Brother-in-Law is a Jerk." Thank you so much. I have ordered some copies through Amazon for Christmas presents.
>   -- Coleman Nee, Yarmouthport, MA

i

What they have said about the
SHORT STORIES
of   Daniel Hoyt Daniels

We read your stories with pleasure; we especially liked "Turkey in the Straw,."
-- Henry and Lois Ross, Nokesville, VA

It is as though O Henry himself were with us again.   Daniels is a master storyteller. Delightful.
-- Ethard Van Stee, Novelist, Beaufort, SC

Made me laugh aloud. You write beautifully. Very clever endings.
-- Mimi Rankin, Vienna, VA

A wonderful collection of stories. You are a wonderful writer. "The Live Oak" is my favorite; it made me cry. Also "Hypocrisy" and "Bastille Day."   "You Took the Words" was lots of fun.
-- Nancy Shaw, Summerfield, FL, formerly Beaufort,SC

We like your stories.   You are a natural writer.   We took turns reading them at La Posada Inn..
-- John Snyder, Laredo, TX

I'm enjoying one at a time.
-- Judy Osborne, Boston, MA

Enjoying your book of stories. Appealing style. I like the fact that each can be enjoyed in a short time. Just right when there's a minute or two when one wants to be productive.
-- John Trask, Beaufort, SC

Très bonne humour. Amusing and philosophical at the same time.
-- Michele Wernert-Piper, New York, NY

You are a gifted writer.
-- Mr. and M rs. Francis Williamson, Beaufort, SC

Entertaining and thought-provoking; you are a word-master; sounds so real and true; a treasure.
-- Peg Flanagan, Beaufort, SC

SHORT STORIES
AT LAST

by

DANIEL HOYT DANIELS

author of

"BAKED ALASKA
AND OTHER
SHORT SHORT STORIES"

with
Whimsy, Humor, and Tongue-in-Cheek
for your
Guestroom Bedside Table

Trade paper Edition 13 digit ISBN: 9781582188744

First DSI Printing: October 2018

Published by Digital Scanning, Inc. Scituate, MA 02066
http://www.Digitalscanning.com

Preface to the third collection, "Short Stories Galore"

These little stories are all fictional works originally written for the amusement and pleasure of the author and his friends. Like the stories in my first two published collections, most of them are completely imaginary, although some of them may have originated from a seed of truth. They can usually be read aloud in ten or fifteen minutes, which is the approximate amount of time that used to be allotted to each participant attending the periodic meetings of the Beaufort Writers' Group. Although the Group is no longer active, I must acknowledge the helpful guidance and encouragement I received there, primarily from Ethard Van Stee, the organizer and stylish director of the Group. The stories are all unrelated to one another. If the same name appears in more than one story, it is not to be implied that it is the same character. The stories are not arranged in any particular order, and appear approximately as they were written chronologically.

I have always appreciated comments and suggestions from many various friends, family, colleagues, and acquaintances, who may see themselves in some of my stories whether in the limelight, twilight, or taillight. I shall neither embarrass you nor swell your egos by calling names, but you know who you are . . . at least some of you do. Thank you.

Any errors are of course my own. Comments on these pieces, or requests for reproduction or other use of them, will be welcomed by the author.

Preface to the fifth collection, "Short Stories Encore"

People sometimes ask me whether a particular story of mine is true or imaginary. The clever reply is of course, "Yes." However, the answer is that each is a mix of truth and imagination, but rarely in equal proportions. Some are almost complete fabrications with only an occasional touch of truth for flavor. A few may be substantially true with but slight embellishment to help the story flow. It would be difficult to say what proportion of any story is truth. On the one hand, truth may sometimes seem quite far fetched and unbelievable; perhaps, in that case, "truth is stranger than fiction." On the other hand, sometimes good fiction can be made to sound very real; perhaps how real it sounds may be one measure of how good it is.

I like to read stories aloud, and, whether they are truth or fiction, I always try to give them as much verisimilitude as possible. Occasionally, after I have read aloud one of my most preposterous and implausible tales, with a smooth voice and a straight face, one of my listeners, with an equally straight face, will come up to me and ask, "Did that really happen?" I am always delighted.

I hope these stories will delight you too. If any one them does not particularly strike your fancy, go on to the next one. It will be different. They are all designed to be read aloud. Read them aloud to each other after you have gone to bed. If they put you to sleep, there is no harm done.

I always welcome comments and suggestions from my readers.

Finally, once again I want to thank Digital Scanning Inc. and Mr. Brian Shillue for their splendid work in the publication of this book and other works of mine.

Winter   Summer

Daniel Hoyt Daniels   or   Daniel Hoyt Daniels
PMB 47, Suite B   PO Box 42
2724 61st Street   Spencertown, NY 12165
Galveston, TX 77551

                                     danielhdaniels@yahoo.com

Introduction

Since he first learned to spell his own name, Daniel Daniels seems to have developed both a singular ability to recognize the humor in human foibles and a pluralistic perception of life's options. Perhaps it was the dual nature of his name, both singular and plural, that inspired Dan to view human interactions against both the choices made and the unmet possibilities not selected.

After a good education and a short service in the military, Dan served in numerous foreign countries as a diplomat in the U.S. Foreign Service. He has innumerable talents that have given his stories depth arising from his careful observations of humanity. He is competent as a sailor, having sailed his 40-foot sloops along the coasts of both Europe and North America. He is a gifted linguist: he has taught Spanish and Italian and has translated several of Molière's plays from the French; accordingly he is conversant in these languages as well as in German. He loves mathematics, classical music and history. And Dan is of course an accomplished author of short stories, with this book being the seventh in the series. Utilizing his keen powers of observation and imagination, he has used his experiences and talents to enliven his stories.

Dan and I have been friends for well over three decades as fellow sailors and explorers of concepts. My family and I have known Dan as a humorous dramatist and actor in his own one-act plays, an enthusiastic debater, and a valued family friend. Sharing his love of classical music with us, he has promoted my daughter's appreciation of listening as well as performing. Similarly, the geometrical puzzles he has designed have entertained me on numerous occasions.

The stories Dan writes are typically poignant vignettes of the human condition. He uses a humorous approach, sometimes with wry pathos, playing with words, occasionally inserting sexual innuendos when least expected. His stories often incorporate incidents from his travels and experiences in the Foreign Service as well as from a vivid imagination. Writing in the vernacular of the characters he portrays, he places the reader on intimate terms with them. Characteristic of his stories is the frequent surprise ending, only occasionally predicted by the perceptive reader. For example, one cannot help but sympathize with both the farmer and his wife in "The Piece of Gold", the first story in his previous book, *Short Stories You'll Love.* Through jealousy, misunderstanding, and poor communication we learn in the final paragraphs that the farming couple have ruined their opportunity to rise from poverty. The reader is left to question his own responses to past situations and ponder the outcomes that other choices might have offered.

In this new book the reader again is brought into the emotional turmoils and attempts at resolving personal anguishes. With innuendos and twists, but with empathy, Dan weaves tales in which we are led to review our own perceptions and decision-making processes. In "What You Don't Know", we are carried into the lives of three people whose needs, desires and alluded actions are seemingly transparent. However, despite the apparent transparency of their lives, the author shows how communication can be easily misinterpreted in order to conform to one's expectations. Seeming transparency is shown to be an illusion, opacifying reality. This story, like others, gives us pause to pose the personal question, "Did I really understand when . . . ?"

In "Arranged Marriage" a fabricated social agency is employed to develop a story of young love. As this story unfolds, we find the couple confronted by an intolerable situation. As a competent raconteur, Dan describes the life-changing decision the heroine makes, which set up the twist of fate in the final passages. We are left wondering "But what if she had . . . ?" or "What if he had . . . ?", leading the reader to introspectively ask the personal question "What if *I* had . . . ?"

Whether or not you are familiar with Dan Daniels's previous stories, you will find this collection eminently readable, enjoyable, memorable, and thought provoking. It will be a challenge to see if you can predict the final developments of the stories by outguessing the author's intriguing endings. Sometimes the reader is offered a choice of endings, giving him the option of selecting the most satisfying one. No matter how you read this collection, whether in one sitting or many, you will find the variety of styles, subjects, flavors, concepts, and characters to be intriguing indeed. Enjoy!

Gordon Sproul, Ph.D.
University of South Carolina
Beaufort, SC

June, 2018

Preface

Avid readers appreciate good writers and you will encounter one of them by reading the short stories written by Daniel Hoyt Daniels. Whether it's grammar, punctuation, spelling, or word usage, he is always spot on. True, you may have to consult the help of a dictionary now and then to confirm the meaning of a particular word, but it's a small price to pay for such a rich and extensive vocabulary he offers his readers.

Writing skills aside, the greater treasure resides in the stories themselves. Filled with surprise endings, the clever use of analogies and historical references, he reminds us of what it is to be human. The spectrum of emotions he covers is so broad that it is likely you will see yourself and the life you have led. You won't be the first to experience a *déjà vu* moment. His perception of human behaviors from humor to despair, kindness to greed, is truly compelling.

Before turning out the bedside light, give yourself a good-night treat. Read one or more of Dan Daniels's wonderful stories. Tonight.

Edward Everett Wendell III,
Orange, Va and Jamestown, NY

July, 2018

Plagiarism

When I was a little kid there were two things I particularly liked. I liked making model airplanes, and I liked writing imaginary stories, when I was old enough to write, that is.

I could already write, some, when I was in the first grade, and in the second grade I wrote a story about a frog that could fly. "Frogs can't fly," said my all-knowing, unimaginative teacher.

"Mine can," I insisted, beginning to taste the power a writer has in his ability to make anybody or anything do whatever he wants them to do. "If ants can fly -- some of them -- and bats, which are just mice with wings, why not frogs?" I insisted.

"You have quite an imagination," she said, and left it at that.

I also liked making paper gliders that could fly, and later real little flying model airplanes made of balsa sticks and tissue paper that came in a kit you could buy for a dollar, way back then. But my family were rather poor when I was growing up, so I didn't get a dollar very often./1

/1 See DEPRESSION DANDELIONS, in *Short Stories You'll Love*, by Daniel Hoyt Daniels, p 77, for a view of a kid during the Depression.

When I got to high school I found I was only so-so in math, but I was very good in English Grammar, Spelling, and Composition. My best friend then was a classmate, Ozzie McCain. Ozzie was good in math and helped me with algebra occasionally, while I helped him in English, explaining why you use the subjunctive in sentences like "If I were you . . ." and the nominative in "It is I . . ." Things like that.

Ozzie had a younger brother, Skipper, who was always just a year behind us in school. I helped Skipper in English too. And because he and Ozzie were from a family that was richer than mine, they would sometimes buy me a sandwich for lunch or pay for the movies we occasionally went to on Saturday afternoon. Skipper was a good athlete and got on the varsity football team when he was a sophomore. But time for practice and trips for games cut into his study time, and he needed some help in English. He needed me. His class required a composition almost every Monday, so at first I helped him with them, and then I just started writing them for him every week, and he would pay me something. It was easier simply to go ahead and write a good little paper than to correct a mediocre one and try to improve upon it. I wrote one essay for him that, as it turned out, was too good. His teacher realized that he never could have written himself -- and accused him of plagiarism. He and I thereupon caught Hell for our collusion and cheating, but I learned a lot from the incident. We were admonished and chastised, but fortunately were not expelled from school, and then when I got to college I remembered Skipper, and it gave me an idea.

That was four years ago -- I'm a senior now at State, majoring, naturally, in English. I still love airplanes though, and I'd like to become an airline pilot, but if that doesn't work out, I'd be perfectly happy being an English teacher, which is where more of my talent lies anyway. But first I had to get through college.

I knew from the beginning that I would have to help myself financially when I got to college, given my family's impecunious position, and would have to wangle a part-time job of some sort.

When I first got here as a freshman, I saw a magazine in the library called *Education Review* with an advertisement for ghost writers. The organization placing the ad said they wanted "Ghost writers for professionally written term papers, theses, dissertations, all subjects, all levels, BS to Ph.D."/2

/2 Even today, there are an astonishing number of organizations offering on-line ghost-writing services: completing homework assignments, producing essays, and composing senior theses and even dissertations for variously desperate, lazy, or disengaged college and graduate students. On the internet one can find enticing offerings from "ON-LINE ASSIGNMENT HELPER," "HOMEWORK FOR ME," "GHOST-WRITER HOMEWORK," "SPEEDY PAPER," "PAPER COACH," "SHADOW WALKER," and many others, some of which apparently produce very efficacious, even if costly, results.

I was not familiar with the term "ghost writer," but I soon realized it meant what I was doing back then with Skipper. My plan suddenly appeared right before me, ready made. I immediately contacted the organization and offered my services as ghost writer for "Creative Writing and related English subjects at all levels." Over the next two years I got several commissions that were very rewarding financially and good experience for me. For the first time in my life I was free from financial worries, and doing what I liked to do, namely, writing and working and living in an academic atmosphere. Some of my clients, or customers, were undergraduates like me, seeking a Bachelor's Degree; several were already in graduate school going for Master's Degrees, and one was even a Ph.D. candidate. Handling these assignments and writing these papers came amazingly easy. Give me a subject, and a suggestion of the style and level of erudition appropriate for the user's situation, and the story popped into my head and out onto paper in no time. I was in my element.

One of the courses I am now taking as a first semester senior is called "Creative Embellishment in the Writing of Historical Novels"; it is being given by an adjunct professor named Howard Cornwall. As I was contemplating how to start preparing my mid-term paper last week, I thought back to a piece I had written a couple of years ago as a ghost writer on the subject of "Ulysses S. Grant and His Confederate Friends." It was a well-researched piece focusing on the buddy-buddy connection Grant had developed during the Mexican War with his comrades-in-arms who, a few years later, were to join the Army of the Confederacy (CSA), but it was rich with creative embellishment./3

4

Creative writing is not always limited to the conception and development of ideas for a story out of whole cloth and the imagination of the writer. It may also include stories that contain a seed of truth, or indeed may be fundamentally true throughout, expertly embellished with humanistic and emotional passions and viewpoints. A number of competent writers have achieved success, even fame, by writing up embellished accounts of actual events, particularly national disasters such as the Galveston hurricane of 1900, the Halifax harbor explosion of 1917, and the collapse of the Air Force's DEW (Distant Early Warning) platform, known as Texas Tower 4, off the coast of New England in 1961./4

My piece on Grant appealed to the emotions of the reader and his sense of justice and understanding in the development of relationships between human beings in unusual circumstances. It was a good paper. I realized that

---

/3 For more on Grant's friendship with CSA General Simon Buckner, with whom he had served as a soldier in the Mexican War, see A CIVIL WAR STORY, in *Short Stories Encore,* by Daniel Hoyt Daniels, page 261.

/4 For an example of the Galveston hurricane (our greatest natural disaster) as historical fiction, see "GALVESTON 1900: SWEPT AWAY," by Linda Crist. For an historical account of the Halifax explosion (the greatest explosion anywhere before Hiroshima) written as fiction, see THE GREAT HALIFAX EXPLOSION, by ,John U. Bacon, and for the story of the Texas Tower 4 disaster and other disasters, see "THE WORLD TO COME," by Jim Shepard.

it would fit nicely with the course I am now taking, and saw no reason not to use it, for myself this time. It was a good example of my work, and I was proud of it.

So I did it. I submitted my paper on Grant for Cornwall's course last Monday. I knew he would like it. Cornwall is not a brilliant person, and is a little slow, but his style is rather like mine, and I think most people would consider him good at what he does. Not a lot of unnecessary descriptive words like Paul Thoreau and William Faulkner, but more attention to the choice of fewer, ideal words, more like Evelyn Waugh or Somerset Maugham or even H. L. Menken. Fewer words but better choices.

I was always comfortable with Cornwall; he recognized the quality of my work, gave me top grades, and I even thought I might like to have his job when he went on to something else, or somewhere else, if I could not make it as an airline pilot. So I was quite surprised when he said this morning, without his usual smile, and with contrived forcefulness, "Bowman, I want to see you in my office at 12:15."

"But Sir," I said. (I still called him "Sir" at that point.) "That's lunchtime."

"You can miss lunch. This is important. You may not want lunch anyway when you hear what I have to say to you," he declared, with an atypically brash and assertive tone to his voice, as he walked on down the hall.

Naturally respectful, but also curious, promptly at 12:15 I pushed through his office door, which was already

6

slightly ajar. Cornwall had adopted an unusually authoritative mien, sitting tensely forward with his palms flat on the desk top, crouching like a tiger ready to spring. "You know plagiarism is grounds for dismissal from this institution of learning," he bellowed from his throne of authority. There was no suggestion of the sarcasm with which he often flavored his usual pontifications.

"Plagiarism? What are you talking about?" I said in understandable surprise and wonder.

"This paper of yours on Grant in Mexico."

"Yes? What about it?"

"I know where you got it."

"Where I got it . . .?" I said rather stupidly. "I wrote it."

"You got it from the University Library records of Master's Degree theses that they keep on file every year."

I thought the man had gone crazy, as I tried to figure out what he was saying. "I did?" I stammered.

"Yes, you did. And you didn't even have the sense to see whose thesis you were copying from. You copied this Grant piece directly from the work of your own Professor of Creative Writing. Thank you for the compliment, but I don't see how anyone could be that stupid."

"Howard," I said -- I didn't even say "Sir" this time -- "Howard, I think you have made a mistake," I said slowly

7

and gently, as I tried to make sense out of this senseless situation. "I don't know how *you* got ahold of the Grant piece, but I originally wrote it on commission for a struggling academic type, someone I never met. I think his name was Hugh Chiswell." I paused momentarily to give my thoughts a moment to catch up with the evolving situation, then continued: "Do you know any Hugh Chiswell, by chance?" I said calmly, as the astounding possibilities were crowding into my stunned head. "Same initials as yours," I added, beginning to smell the truth. "H. C. Interesting, isn't it? Is that just a coincidence?" I said sarcastically, with the true picture now coalescing right before my eyes.

I had been doing the lessons and assignments for my own Professor of Creative Writing as he was working on his Master's Degree! I was stunned, astonished, and quite surprised.

Cornwall was probably even more surprised than I was. He was speechless. Maybe he couldn't think of anything to say, or maybe he was unable to get the words out, with his throat having seized up and closed down completely -- I couldn't tell which. He froze where he was. The color drained from his face. His eyes opened wide -- wide open, unblinking, unfocused, as they stared off into space. His jaw dropped halfway to the floor, and pink saliva started drooling out from a hole in his lower lip that he had bitten in his excitement on hearing the latest news.

"You?" was all he could say. "You, the ghost writer . . .?" he finally stammered. "I never knew," he added, rather unnecessarily, I thought.

8

"I had to," I said, suddenly feeling almost sorry for the miserable wretch there in front of me. "It's my only source of income. But I never would have thought . . ."

"I wouldn't have either," again unnecessarily.

With that, we looked at each other for several minutes, while silence reigned. We were frozen there, just like the subjects of Kipling's famous piece, *East Is East and West Is West*, awaiting God's great judgement. The sudden shock, the realization of the truth, had stunned both of us as we sat there, face to face, dumb, mute, speechless -- brothers under the skin but potentially academic enemies taking advantage of each other, profiting from each other.

"This is . . ." he tried, but had few words. "This is remarkable," he finally managed. True words, I thought, but not very useful./5

"Yes," I said. Usually I say Yes Sir to him, but now I thought that was no longer necessary. "Yes, remarkable." More silence.

/5 In the midst of the blanketing silence there, an old story, just a joke really, crossed my mind. It was about the pilot of a little plane flying from Germany to England above the cloud banks common over the North Sea. With no landmarks in view, he said to his co-pilot and navigator, "Where are we?" The co-pilot simply replied, "We are over the clouds." "You sound like an economist," answered the pilot, "what you say may be true, but it isn't very useful." Ha ha.

9

My mixed feelings and emotions at that moment were colored by a tinge of enjoyment on seeing Cornwall now in such a different light -- no longer the proud, always right, infallible master of the situation, but suddenly a humble, frightened being, looking more like a lad who had been stealing from the cookie jar or driving without a license.

"What are you going to do?" I finally heard him say. It looked as though his big white eyeballs were what was doing the talking.

The question surprised me, for I had not had time to think of doing anything. Not yet. But it also suggested to me that I should indeed start thinking again, for I was going to have some choices to consider.

I certainly did not want to have to face presumptive plagiarism charges that could form a circumstantially strong, albeit falsely founded, case against me. At big educational institutions like this, altercations between students and faculty are invariably, or almost invariably, judged and resolved in favor of the faculty member. And even if I won the case, as I felt sure I would, there could be a detrimental cloud hanging over any career I might have in the eyes of Academia for years to come.

I hesitated a moment, and then began to realize what he meant, and it gave me ideas. Cornwall was afraid I would "turn him in," or expose his crafty academic chicanery.

I had to say something, although I would have liked more time for more thinking. So I said, "I don't know."

10

Cornwall must have taken these non-committal words as a threat, for he then leaned forward and said, in a confidential tone, "Maybe we can work something out."

Ideas began rushing through my head, as I looked at him, sitting forward in his chair, still externally dapper-looking in his custom-made tweed suit and Italian silk necktie. His right arm lay across the edge of the great desk, palm upturned this time, with his shirt cuff revealing his monogrammed gold cuff links.

In case I hadn't mentioned it, Howard Cornwall came from a wealthy family of businessmen that had built up a multi-billion-dollar commercial empire based on the foresight of Howard's great great grandfather, who invented a process for making breakfast cereal flakes out of corn. The product became known as "corn flakes," and was very profitable indeed. Whereas most of his close relatives were still involved in the financial empire, Howard had apparently been touched by a particular teacher in his youth and had decided he wanted to become a teacher himself, flouting the family tradition of money-making. He also had plenty of money himself, of course, and realized that there were other people who envied him his good fortune, as it were.

I suddenly saw what he had in mind. Money. It's money that he has in mind. He has more money than he needs, even if it is family money. And I have a greater *dearth* of money than *I* need. And he knows that too.

My choices began to crystalize before me:

11

I could turn him in and probably win my case against the plagiarism accusation without too much trouble, and at the same time win him for a lifetime mortal enemy.

I could confess to the plagiarism charge, leave college without my degree, and keep him for an everlasting friend, while living in financial comfort for the rest of my life on the great chunk of Cornwall's family fortune that I could see his eyeballs offering me, even now. He was hoping I would accept an astronomical pile of money in exchange for my cooperation, I mean in exchange for my silence, and surrender to his nefarious career ambition.

Great Guns! What a choice!

I would have to think about it.

THE END

Christmas Gifts

"What did you get for Christmas?"

"I got to go to Colorado."

"I mean, what did you get for a Christmas present?"

"Going to Colorado was my Christmas present."

"Why would you want to go to Colorado? -- what's so great about that?"

"I got a chance to visit my grandmother out there and tell her that I loved her."

"Where does she live in Colorado?"

"She used to live in Boulder, but she doesn't live there anymore. She died soon after Christmas, on January 6."

"Oh. So I guess your trip was pretty much wasted. That couldn't have been much fun for you."

"Yes it was, and my trip wasn't wasted. It wasn't wasted at all. When I told her I loved her, she smiled at me. She had a beautiful smile, although she didn't talk much this time. But she did smile. I'll bet she is still smiling on us now. She used to take me for walks in the woods when I was little. She said that the woods were like paradise, and

13

when I asked her what 'paradise' meant, she said she thought it meant heaven. Now I guess she knows for sure. Anyway, I still think of her whenever I'm in the woods, and sometimes in other places too."

"I've never been in the woods much."

"You might like it. There are a lot of woods around Boulder, and when it snows the woods are really beautiful. Every pine tree and spruce tree and fir tree is like a Christmas tree, only even prettier. They don't have to have tinsel on them or presents under them to be Christmas-y. That's what my grandmother said too, and she knew everything."

"Sounds cool."

THE END

Arranged Marriage

Someone once said there are things we can control and things we cannot control, and we should pray to God for wisdom to tell the difference. I've tried that, but it doesn't always work.

A long time ago, when I was a child, it didn't work at all. I never seemed to have any control or any choices whatsoever. I could not even choose which thumb to suck, my right thumb or my left thumb. The fact is that I wasn't allowed to suck either one of them. Why did God give them to us anyway, right there in such a convenient location, if we weren't supposed to suck them?

You see, I was born in the Old Country, back when times were different. In those days, in our village and certainly in our family, religion and tradition were the most important things in life. Religion told us what to do, and tradition told us how to do it. Fortunately it was not always exactly like that. It was my father that did both of those things -- told us what to do and how. He was the Lord of the Castle and his word was Law.

My father loved his children -- I'm sure he did -- but he never really liked us. The Bible says that children must love and obey their parents; maybe it also says somewhere that parents should love their children. But he would whip us for taking a cookie between meals and then put his arms around us and tell us how much he loved us and how sorry he was that we had to be whipped.

15

There were only two children in our family, my older sister, Greta, and me. I'm Ingrid. Two girls, unfortunately, as Father saw it. Father always wanted a son, because that was somehow the important thing in his traditional culture. He used to scold Mumsie and beat her for not giving him a son, although to me in my childish innocence that seemed counter productive and unlikely to produce the desired result. Greta and I trembled under his rigorous authority. He had to decide what clothes we could wear, what hats (little white religious bonnets) we could have, what food, what books, what pets, what school, what friends. Plus dozens of things we could *not* have or could not do. No apples (sinful), no male friends (sinful), no dancing (sinful), no waste of paper, scraps, or uneaten food (financial profligacy), no movies (sinful and profligate). And dozens of other restrictions.

Greta and I were dutiful. Always accepting, always obeying, always trying to please or at least satisfy Father, keep peace in the house, and avoid his periodic outbursts and beatings to the extent possible.

In short we had a tough upbringing and childhood. Today we probably would have been called abused children.

When Greta was 18 and out of high school, Father arranged her marriage to a fellow named Serge Krowsky, someone she didn't even know, but who was supposed to make a good husband for her because *his* father was a friend of Father's. As it turned out, Serge pushed her around and beat her just as much as Father had ever done. When she gave birth to a daughter, neither Serge nor Father was at all pleased; both wanted succession in the male line, and Greta was scolded, berated, and chastised for her shortcoming. To make matters worse, the birth had been difficult and the doctors had to tell Greta, or rather Greta's husband and father, that Greta could never have any more children. Greta's chastisement only increased with the continuation of vociferous diatribes replete with expressions like "worthless bitch" and "useless woman," as they say in English.

I haven't mentioned that my best friends at this time were two high school classmates of Greta's: Petrina Gorsky and Pieter Conrad. These two also came from religious families and went to the same church we did. The two were very different from each other; they had met once or twice in church, but that's about all.

Petrina was violently opposed to marriage of any sort, arranged or not, and swore she would never marry, as all she had ever seen was ugliness, animosity, and suffering arising therefrom. Even before Father arranged Greta's marriage to Serge, Petrina learned that *her* father had gotten the same idea. Petrina had also suffered a rough upbringing as a child. She wasn't going to marry anyone, especially some guy she didn't even know. Accordingly, one dark night Petrina slipped away and went to Australia. It wasn't so simple as I make it sound: she had been planning it for several months and it was a difficult trip for her, but that's a different story.

Petrina was indiscreet enough to write to me telling me to promise I would never let her parents or anyone else know where she had gone. So of course I promised. She also told me there were a lot of eligible single men around Adelaide in South Australia where she was, and a reasonably nice-looking woman with a pair of arms and a pair of legs and a pair of a few other things, like eyes and ears, could take her pick from the bunch. She had already met a man she liked, although she "certainly hadn't married him." She wasn't sure she wanted to "go that far" just yet.

I wrote back to her, thanking her for her news and telling her what was going on back here. I told her what was happening to Greta. I also told her I was having a romance -- my very first romance -- with my friend Pieter Conrad -- "do you remember him?"

It was more than just a romance between Pieter and me. I loved Pieter; I had fallen in love with him, heart and soul. He is so different from any other boys or men I have known -- different from *anybody* else. "He is a God-fearing person, Petrina. He goes to church regularly, and follows our religious teaching: a loving and caring person. And he cares for *me*. I am the only one he could love. He told me that. He said so. Some men . . . I don't believe anything they say. But not Pieter. I believe him. I would do anything for him. I would marry him in a minute. I *will* marry him." I put all that in my letter to Petrina.

Then something happened.

I wrote to Petrina again, telling her about it.

The next time I saw Pieter it was not for our usual fun and games, and the deep satisfaction he regularly gave me when we were together. When I saw him the eventful

18

afternoon, he was wearing a long pallid face, longer than anything else I had ever seen. "Oh my Darling," I said, throwing myself into his arms, "has something happened?" For I could see that something had happened.

"Something has happened," he said quite seriously. "We have to stop seeing each other."

"Stop seeing each other?" I stammered, aghast. "What on Earth are you talking about? What in God's name are you saying?" He tried to back off, peeling my clenched grips from his humeri, and taking his eyes off me for the first time ever.

"I'm getting married," he said. "It wasn't my idea," he added, unnecessarily I thought -- I hoped. "My father is arranging it all."

"Pieter," I almost screamed, "you are 21! You don't have to do this! You don't have to do everything your father says."

"Yes, I know, my Dear," he said, still looking at the floor and twisting his fingers together like a little boy. "But this I have to do. The Bible tells us to honor thy father and thy mother. He is my father."

I had to sit down and catch my breath in silence. My Darling? My Love? My Pieter getting married? Married to *someone else*? How can I go on living without him?

"I won't go on living without you," I said, trying to speak slowly and quietly.

19

"What?"

"Arranged marriages are only a formality. We don't have to stop seeing each other."

"What! What are you saying? That would be . . . would be Adultery!"

"It happens all the time. You are my real husband -- my husband in the flesh. I'm not committing adultery. If anyone is, it's that other woman who will be committing adultery, not me. What's her name, anyway?"

"Her name?"

"Yes, her name. What's her name . . . ? She has a name, hasn't she?"

"I . . . I don't know . . . I'll find out."

"*Um Gottes Willen!* You'll find out . . . ! And what am I supposed to do?" Silence.

"I'm sorry. It's this religious thing and traditional family values that I have been brought up with. I wish it were different. I really do."

With each of his words my fury doubled. "You cad! Deceitful cad! Faithless scoundrel! I hate you! I hate you!"

"But Ingrid, Darling, I love you."

20

"A fine way you have of showing it! I never want to see you again!" With that I stormed out and went back home where I should have stayed in the first place. I had to stop and rest along the way, and try to catch my breath and gather together the broken pieces of my heart and soul. I couldn't let even my parents see me in my outrageously distraught and disheveled condition.

"Where have you been?" said my mother. "What's happened to you? You look outrageously distraught and disheveled." You see, my mother always wants to know everything I do.

"I went for a walk. A walk in the woods."

"You look like you met the three bears head on," she said, laughing at her own humor. "Well, I have made us supper, so you can wash the dishes." Fine. That's fine, I thought. Back to the old routine. And Sunday we will all go to church, and I will pray for guidance and try to learn whether there is anything in this life that I can change or make sense of.

*   *   *   *   *

It was only a week later that my father declared one evening, "I've been thinking of you, my Darling . . ." Frightening words. I girded my loins and crossed my fingers. "You have been looking rather sad and lonely lately. And I know the reason," he declared most positively. "You are lonely," he said. "Without a man in your life, you are lonely."

Wow! I was suddenly taken aback. Does he know about me and Pieter? Can he be that perspicacious? Does he realize I have lost the love of my life? No, that can't be. If he knew I had been carrying on with a man and was no longer a virgin, he would have hit the ceiling and given me the whipping of my life, although I am 19 years old. No, that's not it. What is it then? "I'm all right," I said, perfunctorily.

"I have good news for you." Again, the shudder returned.

"And . . .?"

"I have arranged for your marriage. It is time you settled down and behaved and quit going for walks in the woods all the time."

"Oh, Father! I'm only nineteen, and I'm not interested in marriage anyway!"

"You're just the right age, and it's all settled. I have been working on it for several weeks. He is a very nice young man, and his father is a friend of mine."

"Father, no! I can't get married!"

"No? Why not?"

"I . . . I . . . " I was grasping at straws; I had to come up with something. "I'm too young," I stammered . . . "And besides . . . uh . . . I think I'm a Lesbian."

"That's Tommyrot. You have all the necessary equipment in all the right places. Anyway, you can bear me a grandson whether you're a Lesbian or not. Lesbians do it all the time -- or at least sometimes -- although usually it is before they realize they are Lesbians. Being a Lesbian is just in your mind. Your body is fine. Now it's all settled. The wedding will be a week from Saturday."

"Oh, Father!"

"And that's that," he growled.

*   *   *   *   *

I had to do some thinking, so I started thinking. If this had happened two months ago, I would have tried to persuade Pieter to run off with me somewhere. Maybe America. Maybe Australia. Yes, that's it! Australia! If Petrina could do it, why can't I? She was barely 21 and I'm a smart 19. I'll go to Australia!

Petrina had told me how she did it. She had gotten her visa at the Australian Consulate in Venice, and then arranged with the Cavendish Agency there for a loan and financial aid for travel expenses.

The Cavendish Agency was one of the first match-making agencies ever established on an international scale. They would advance funds for a woman willing to go to Australia for marriage to one of the many single men there. Under the terms of the typical arrangement, if the woman did not find a man sufficiently to her liking within one year, she had to reimburse the financial advance and pay her own way back to her country of origin.

23

It was a win-win, no lose situation, and I thanked the Lord that Petrina was my friend as I silently packed one small suitcase with a minimum of essentials: toothbrush, lipstick, comb, douche bag, face powder, deodorant, change of clothes including an extra brassiere (I'd bought a cute, cheap one at the Bazaar last summer, but it didn't hold up very well) and two pair of shoes -- low heels for walking and high heels for strutting about and lying down. I took all the money from a can I had been saving in the bathroom, and all the money from a can that Mumsy had been saving in the kitchen -- which was supposed to be for my education or dowry or something. I had no qualms about taking it. This trip to Australia would certainly be educational, and if I had a little change left over toward a dowry, so much the better. I wrote her a note, saying "Don't worry, Mumsy, this is the last money I will ever take from you." I signed it "Love, Ingrid," and stuck it back in the can.

* * * * *

And that's about the way it worked out. I slipped out of the house when no one was looking, caught a bus to Venice, contacted the Australian Consulate and the Cavendish Agency office down by the docks, and took passage on the next vessel heading for the Far East. It happened to be the *Empress of Australia,* a vessel of the British White Star Line on a round-the-world cruise. I was lucky; I got a cheap berth that had become vacant because at the last minute one of the passengers had to cancel plans in Venice and return to England for an emergency. Well, my case was an emergency too, I thought to myself, as they checked me in.

I got the ship's nice radio operator to send a message to Petrina telling her I was on my way. Three and a half weeks later she and her Australian husband met me in Adelaide. Quite a thrill to see her again, happy there in her new life, with no parents or religious mantra telling her what to do.

I met several of her husband's friends as well as several others through the Cavendish Agency office in Adelaide. Some of them were quite attractive if I do say so myself. Although my mind had been severely tainted by men, my body felt otherwise, having known Pieter rather well, as it were. By then it was a good while since I had touched a man, and the opportunities were suddenly very inviting. In short, I let myself fall in love with the first man I met. His name was Michael Henderson. Maybe I was on the rebound. So what. My body needed him even if I didn't.

All that was eight years ago. Now I am Ingrid Henderson -- Mrs. Michael Henderson. My husband is a good man who lets me read anything I want to read and doesn't whip me if I eat cookies or miss church or forget to put the cat out. Father finally got a male descendant, although he never knew it. We have two boys, 6 and 4, and live on a farm, or "property," several miles from Adelaide. Our place is called Williwena, which means "dry sand" or something like that in one of the aboriginal languages. There is a lot of work for me here. Mostly we raise sheep, but I also take care of the boys, tend the vegetable garden, take care of the chickens and the other chores. Good household help is practically non-existent. Anybody around here that is at all competent seems already to have a job, or else is busy taking care of a place of his own./1

25

It is not an easy life, but I am in good health and I have a sincere and hard-working husband whom I like very much, even if I cannot say I truly love him. That only happens once. True love, I mean. At least in my case. I once loved, loved and cherished -- Pieter was his name -- years ago, with a love that could never be replaced. I tried not to think of Pieter anymore or how he suddenly dumped me out of respect for his religion and the word of his father. Oh, how I hated him! But I loved him! And I never could forget him no matter how hard I tried to hate him.

So that's the way things were with me, and that's the way they stayed for some years, there in the Outback of Australia.

Then one day something happened.

* * * * *

One bright spring afternoon in October there came a knock on the door. I was alone in the house; Mike was out working on the fences and the children were playing with our newest lambs.

I opened the door, and you won't believe who I saw there. I could hardly believe it myself. It was Pieter. There he was, standing in front of me, with his hands by his sides and an uncontrollable smile crossing his lips. I couldn't

---

/1 For more on the opportunities and rigors of outback life in South Australia, see *A Faraway Place in the Sun*, by Elizabeth Haran.

have been more surprised if it had been his ghost, and for a second I almost wondered what it was I was seeing there. My first impulse was to throw myself into his arms, but I suddenly remembered that I was married, and that this was the man who betrayed me, the man who had broken my heart, the man who had turned me down, the man I hated now. I pondered all these things for about two seconds.

I didn't know whether to throw myself into his arms or not, so I went ahead and threw myself into his arms, as I was going to do in the first place. It was a while before I could think of anything to say, or could have said, choked up as I was. Finally I managed to stammer something:

"What are you doing here?"

"I had to see you."

"You'd better come in. I'll make some tea," I said perfunctorily without thinking. Then, shaking all over: "Why on Earth would you want to see me after all these years . . .? You're a married man and must have a dozen children."

"No, I'm not married. I have never been married. No children either."

What is he saying? I was nonplussed, completely stunned. I knew he had accepted an arranged marriage and tossed me out the window.

"What on Earth are you saying?" I blurted out. "You accepted an arranged marriage and tossed me out the window. Why couldn't you have at least called or written that you were coming? How did you find me anyway? Oh, Pieter!" I said with my heart and my feelings all stirred up and confused as they silently screamed at me and at each other from within. It's a good thing I was sitting down. I thought I might faint, but I knew that wouldn't have done any good. I had to use my head to sort out this tangle of overwhelming emotions that were engulfing me.

"I was afraid that if you knew I was coming you might say no. Of course you would say no, and you would be justified in doing so because of the way I treated you -- because of what I did to you. I have lived in pain and sorrow, and remorse and contrition, for years now, with the grisly memory of that eventful day hanging around my neck like an albatross, never letting go, as it dominated my thoughts and feelings constantly. I could never care for another woman as I cared for you. As I *do* care for you."

"Don't say that, Pieter. I'm married too now. But how can it be that *you* are not married? That was the whole thing."

"When the time came for our wedding, the father of the would-be bride came shuffling apologetically to us to report the horrible news that the bride-to-be had run away. I never knew who the bride was; never knew her name until three months later when her father died. People talked about it at the funeral. It was just after my own father died. And that's when I learned who her father was."

"All right, so what? What's that got to do with me?"

"It's this, Ingrid," he said, gently laying his hand on my forearm and looking with tearful eyes into my own eyes as he had once done so many years ago . . . "It's this: her father was *your* father. I had never known the name of the girl I was supposed to marry, the one who ran away. It was you, Ingrid. I was supposed to marry *you*. That was the arranged marriage."

"Oh, my!"

THE END

Epilogue

Pieter went on to explain a few things: "My father died before he could arrange another marriage for me. And I have never looked at another woman. I spent years trying to find out where you were, but you left no tracks. I had no idea you were in Australia. Then just a few weeks ago by chance I ran into Petrina, who was back home for a visit. I didn't even recognize her at first, but she recognized me, and she is the one who told me where you were. And that's how I got here. I just had to see you. Once, at least. But I don't want to interrupt anything: I am glad to see you are happy here with your Australian family . . . I'll be leaving now . . ."

"Oh, Pieter . . ."

"Yes?"

"Pieter, I . . ."

THE FINAL END

Slavery, Anyone?

It is surprising, how surprising some people are, that you can meet in surprising places, and the surprising things you might find yourselves talking about.

I am thinking about a time one January when I was on a tiny Caribbean island, way out of the way, definitely off the beaten track. I was rather surprised to meet a Swedish lady, right there on the beach. She had come all the way from Stockholm to enjoy the Caribbean sunshine, when she could have gotten the same thing, or almost the same thing, in the Canary Islands, or Senegal, or Yemen, or some place on the Red Sea which was only half as far away from home.

She was comfortably ensconced in the shade behind a giant beech umbrella -- canopy really -- and deeply engaged in a paperback novel, as many sunbathers and vacationers sometimes are. As I came out of the ocean I had to pass fairly near the lady on my way back to my towel, so I started thinking of something to say in case she caught my eye. The gentleman should always speak first, of course. The sunshine? Too trite. The water? *Deja vu* all over again. Ah, the book! I'll ask her what she is reading.

"Hello, there, what are you reading?" I said. "I see that you have a book," I added, rather unnecessarily, to forestall the inexorable return of obdurate silence, and hoping to receive a word from her in return. And, indeed, I was successful!

"Yes," she said, "a book."

Well, that sounded like a positive answer, so I pressed on: "What's it about?" I asked, trying to show polite interest.

"None of your business," she would have been justified in saying, but didn't.

"People," she said, because Swedes have a reputation of being polite. Then, apparently thinking that that sounded a bit curt, she added, "It's about slavery."

"Oh, about slavery in Brazil?" I said, trying to act a bit smart, for our island wasn't far from the northern coast of Brazil, and I had recently read that almost ten times more slaves were shipped from Africa to Brazil than were ever brought into the American Colonies or the United States.

"No, the United States."

So I said, "I have read that almost ten times more slaves were shipped from Africa to Brazil than were ever brought into the American Colonies or the United States," showing off my knowledge.

"Really?"

THE END

What You Don't Know

What you don't know won't hurt you. That's what they say. And maybe what other people don't know won't hurt you either, as long as you are sure they don't know.

Take the case of Harriet Mahoney, for instance -- what happened to her -- and you will see what I mean.

They were a happy married couple -- Harriet and Conrad -- happier than most anyway. Married for three decades and still in love. But by now they were getting on in years, especially Harriet, who was only seven and a half years younger than Conrad. The fact is that, by the time she hit fifty, Harriet was beginning to get a little tired of romance.

Harriet liked solitude too; liked being alone with her thoughts. That was about the time she began writing stories. Fiction, mostly, simple imaginings. Her best friend, June Richter, was a woman she knew from church, whose husband traveled a lot. Harriet envied her friend, who had a great deal of time alone, and June envied Harriet, who had a husband who was so romantic. Sometimes when June's husband, Eric, was away, the other three had supper together. Harriet would let June and Conrad talk on, while she only half listened. Harriet liked to muse and contemplate, wherever she was, and ponder her next story, whether she was at the dinner table, or in the shower, or in her back garden. She liked having her friend June divert her husband's attention -- get him off her back occasionally, so to speak.

33

She didn't mind seeing them go off to the movies sometimes after supper; it gave her more time alone. She didn't mind Conrad's spending Sunday afternoons at June's place. It just meant more time for her herself.

One afternoon, when June was over at Harriet's place, before Conrad got home, she outright said to Harriet, "Harriet, there is something I ought to tell you."

"Yes, and what is that?"

"It's Conrad."

"Conrad?" replied Harriet, suddenly afraid that June was going to complain that Conrad had been annoying her, or abusing her, or possibly even molesting her.

"Yes, Conrad."

"What about Conrad?" said Harriet, now quite nervous.

"It's just . . ."

"Yes, just what?"

"It's just that I like Conrad."

"Yes, I knew that," said Harriet, now feeling a little more comfortable.

"I mean, I like him a lot."

"Yes, I know that too," said Harriet, now quite relieved.

"I am trying to tell you that I like being with him."

"That's nice . . . that's fine," said Harriet, no longer worried. "He likes being with you too, and I think I have told you how happy I am that he does. You mean a lot to him. I love him dearly, but I just don't have enough time and energy to give him all the attention he likes to have; I need more solitude than he does -- more quiet time to myself. He really needs company and companionship almost constantly, you know. So what I am saying is that I do appreciate the way your friendship with Conrad has given me more time to do the writing and contemplation that I feel I have to do by myself. Please don't change a thing. I love knowing that you and Conrad are happy together; it makes me happy too."

"You are a dear to say those sweet things. You mean you are not jealous when I see Conrad?"

"Jealous? Me? Of course not. I am delighted. Conrad and I see each other enough even so -- you don't have to worry about that."

All this was just what June wanted to hear. June loved her own husband, Eric, but she was a gregarious person who needed a lot of companionship, just like Conrad needed a lot of companionship. They had no desire to hurt their spouses or anyone else, and would have kept their growing friendship, or even love, silent and hidden. However, June was elated to know that Harriet did not mind her seeing Conrad, and even seemed to endorse and

35

encourage the two being together. She must know that we are romantically involved, thought June, after Harriet had given her such support when they talked about it. June felt quite relieved, glad that she had opened up honestly, as she was not a person who would have liked having to hide her feelings, or her lovers either, if she ever had any.

That situation went on for many months, which turned into years, as the relationship between Conrad and June only deepened.

One day Conrad got one of those promotional phone calls, telling him he was a lucky winner of two tickets for a Caribbean cruise. All he had to do was spend a day in a Fort Lauderdale suburb enjoying a guided tour of a new upscale gated community development. On previous occasions, when offered such advertising come-ons, he had slammed down the receiver, but, for no reason at all, this time he decided to pursue it and see if there really was a Santa Claus and a free Caribbean cruise in the offing. After filling out numerous forms, and answering many questions, and compliantly looking at dozens of real estate opportunities, he was told he was one of ten finalists. He stuck with it, and after many more questions and a couple more visits he was one of the three winners. He now had two tickets for a ten-day cruise from Lauderdale to Yucatan, Belize, Cayman Islands, and return. He excitedly gave his wife Harriet the good news and told her to get herself ready, but she didn't like the idea too much. "I have no desire to climb into one of those Norwegian cruise ships packed with 3,000 other people, just as though it were a cheap chain hotel. I have plenty to do here," she said. "Why don't you ask June? Her husband will be in Australia until February. She might be willing to go along with you, if you want companionship."

Well, would you believe, Conrad was thinking the same thing. Now, don't get me wrong. He loved his wife, but there were aspects of his life that June seemed more capable of filling, and more interested in, than his dear Harriet did. Harriet always appreciated every free minute of time he could give her for herself. Ten days of quiet for her would be a welcome godsend.

June told Conrad that Harriet knew all about their little love affair, and that Harriet had no objection. Conrad of course had been too discreet to discuss it openly with Harriet, but June could do so. Woman talk. Women can tell one another things that even married couples cannot tell each other.

"You mean, she doesn't mind even if we, you know, do things?" said Conrad.

"You silly boy. Of course she doesn't. She knows all about it. About us. As long as we don't blab about it to all the world, it's fine with her. Hasn't she ever told you she likes having more time to herself for her writing and contemplation?"

"Well, yes, but . . . Actually, I was hoping that that was the case, but I never had the nerve to broach it to her so blatantly. But I really am delighted that she does know, and that it's all right with her. You know, I love her dearly, but maybe you also know that there really isn't much romance between us."

"Yes, my Dear, I have known that for many months."

So Conrad told June about the tickets he had won for the cruise, and she got quite interested. "Do you think they will have double beds on the *Norwegian Sea Queen*? Or are all the berths -- or whatever they call them — single bunks?"

"I'm sure the ship people have worked it out and know what they are doing," he replied a bit vaguely. "Maybe all of them are single bunks that you can strap yourself into so you don't fall out if the ship begins to rock and roll at night. Ha ha!"

So they did it. They went on the nice cruise. The ship went to Yucatan, Belize, and the Cayman Islands, just as was promised. Pleasant cruise. There weren't even any surprises.

As soon as they got back, Conrad threw his arms about his wife, bubbling over to tell her all about the trip. He looked healthy, a little sun tanned, and certainly full of good spirits. She too was feeling in good health, relaxed and rested after her quiet week with her writings and contemplations.

"We had glass-bottom boats to see the coral reefs and tropical fish at Cozumel," he told her eagerly, "and a visit to a native village in Belize, and we ate conch fritters by a campfire on the beach in the Cayman Islands, where all the rich bankers go."

"I'm so glad you had a good time," said Harriet, picturing her dear husband in pleasant surroundings. Then out of curiosity, and wondering how comfortable it would have been, she asked, "and how were your quarters? Did you have to sleep in bunks, like sailors, one on top of the other?"

"Oh, no -- nothing like that," he replied, barely restraining a smile, as a picture of her metaphor crystalized before his eyes. "They were just regular beds; they only call them bunks to sound more seaman-like. Look, I have some photographs of our cabin and the rest of the ship as well. I thought we could make some copies and send them around to family and friends who might be interested."

"Yes, that would be nice. Here, let me see . . . Oh, I love this one of the bow wave . . . And this must be coming into Cozumel. My parents took me there when I was 16, and I still remember it . . . And this one of you and June and the Captain. Wow! And here, even the swimming pool. They're all lovely . . . And what's this one? Oh, it must be the inside of your cabin; that's the porthole. And there's the corner of one of your beds. It looks pretty big. Were both of your beds that big?"

"Well, no. I asked for two single beds," he lied, "but the double was what came with the special offer, and by then it was all they had available. So we had to make do with just the one bed."/1

/1 Actually it was the other way around. There was in fact more demand for double beds than there was for singles.

"All right, I can understand that," she said, giving Conrad another welcoming hug. "But Darling," she said, "you can't send these pictures all over everywhere."

"Why not? What's wrong with them?"

"Well, this picture of your cabin -- it shows quite clearly that there's a double bed in there. You can't let that get around; what would people think?"

THE END

God's Little Helper

"Gawd Aaaaw-maah-tee!" someone said. The words were loud and clear, five by five, with a slight Southern accent. At first it wasn't clear whether it was an oath, or a call for help, or merely a question. However, it was neither of these. It was an attention getter, meaning, "Hey God, look over here!"

It seems the fellow was a census taker for the US Government, currently working in southern Alabama on a regular periodic ten-year project. But he was a thoughtful person, as well as an assiduous and honest worker, and he let his thoughts wander back over a few years -- many years in fact . . .

* * * * *

God was tired. He had been working hard all week, creating the earth and the sky, and the sun and the moon, and the planets and the stars. And then the mountains and the oceans, and the fish and frogs and trilobites. And then the rocks and rills and templed hills, plus shrubs and flowers, and orange trees and pear trees -- and of course apple trees -- to make it all beautiful and tasteful.

By then He was very tired, but He still had to find someone or something to watch over His creation and care for the earth and its ecology and enjoy its beauty. So he decided to make a man. He scraped together some dust

41

that no one was using, shaped it more or less into the form of His own self, blessed it and breathed on it, and when it came to life, called it Adam. "Adam" was an old Aramaic word that God remembered from his religious studies, meaning "*first man*," so naturally God thought that would be a good name for Adam to have.

Now that God had created a Man to take care of the Earth, he realized he needed someone to take care of Man, to boss him around and try to tell him what to do. So he decided to create Woman.

But God was really tired now: you can't imagine how much work it is to create a living person out of dust. So to make a second person, God took an easier way out. He took one of Adam's ribs, a piece of living flesh and bone -- bone mostly -- and made a woman out of that. Much easier than using dust. Then He sat back for a minute and admired His handiwork. "Not bad," He thought, "but we could use some more creatures like this Adam and Eve; the Earth is pretty big and needs a lot more than two people to populate it and take care of it."

But, like I said, God was tired. It was a lot of work just making one man out of dust and one woman out of a rib. "Besides," thought God, "I'm getting old. I am going to have to learn to take it easy if I am going to live forever."

* * * * *

Now while all this was going on, the Devil was closely following the action with his supernatural powers of ESP plus some of the latest ungodly bugs and listening devices that he had devilishly rigged up all over Heaven and Earth. He was awaiting his chance. He was looking for a chink in God's armor and his protective entourage of angels and cherubim. He saw that God was tired and seemed to need help, and realized that that would give him an advantage that he should take advantage of.

"God Almighty," hollered the Devil to get the Creator's attention. Now God knew he was almighty, but he didn't know that anyone else knew it, so he replied, "Yes? Is someone calling me? Who is it?"

"It is I, your good friend the Devil," came the answer.

"Have we met?" asked God, "I didn't know the Devil was my friend. Are you sure you're the Devil?"

"Oh yes, I'm quite sure. And it's time for us to meet. I think we should cooperate -- you know, like, help each other."

"What did you have in mind?"

"I have a plan that will, like, make it easy for you to populate the Earth," said the Devil, his eyes full of mischief and lambent fire. "That's what you want to do, isn't it?"

"Well, yes, but I wouldn't want anybody to have to sin to do it."

"For God's sake, God! You have to let people sin a little to get them to do what you want them to do. No man nowadays wants to give up a perfectly good rib and have it

43

taken from his side to make a woman; he would rather use something else and do it a different way."

"How do you know all this?"

"I'm a sinner, remember? You have to make it pleasant and fun for Adam and Eve and other people on Earth to make babies and propagate the race, if you really want it to work. What you should do is give them a little exquisite enjoyment in the process, and your difficulties are overcome and your problems are solved. People will love (Ha ha) to propagate throughout the world if you make the procedure enough fun for them, and if you also let them know that fornication is a sin. There is nothing that people will enjoy more than the pleasure of knowing they are sinning, and pleasuring themselves at the same time."

"How should I get this started? Tell me how to go about it, if you have such great ideas."

"Let Eve have a bite of the next apple that falls for her. Apples and other fruits are always falling for pretty girls. Now by that I certainly don't mean the fruity homosexuals you may be thinking of. I just mean fruity guys that are so obsessed by a woman's good looks and charms that they don't know what they are getting into, if you know what I mean. Believe me, they will go ahead and do almost any crazy thing. Love is blind, you know. People think that what you can't see won't hurt you, but you and I know differently, don't we?"

* * * * *

What neither the Devil nor God expected to see was how well the Devil's plan for helping populate the Earth worked out. The results of the Plan were better than anyone ever anticipated or imagined possible. About six thousand years later, one day God said, "You're a little Devil."

"Yes, I know," the Devil replied.

With all the rendezvousing and fooling around and trysts and free love and pairing up and coupling and linking and wild living – and carrying-on that the Devil's plan brought so vigorously into the life of Mankind, the population of the Earth increased by leaps and bounds. Recently, just in one man's lifetime, the population of the Earth increased from 1.8 billion to almost 8 billion. "Gawd Aaaaw-maah-tee!" said the census taker when he realized how well the Devil's population-expansion plan was working. But with the good news came some bad news: a new problem had burst upon the scene. Unfortunately the Earth cannot produce enough apples to feed that many people, and horses like apples too. People must start eating each other. Or else starve. There is no other answer.

"You're a little Devil," said God once more. "You will destroy everything this way."

"Yes, I know," the Devil replied with a smug smile, as he sat back and surveyed his handiwork. "You're right. Over population is devilish. As you say, it is indeed destructive. It will bring about the end of Mankind -- the end of your world," he chuckled.

THE END

Chemistry

Once upon a time there was a young couple that fell in love, both for the first time. The time was the middle of the 22nd century, and by then people had learned not to rush into romantic relationships in the foolhardy fashion so common in earlier centuries. Teen-age pregnancy was no longer popular, and many were holding off on the husband-wife thing until marriage.

She was two years older than her boyfriend, although they both were only in their early twenties, but they were so in love they couldn't wait. They went ahead and did the business. Now the lady had a younger brother who liked to play tricks on people, especially for fun. He thought it would be amusing to play a trick on the fellow, his brother-in-law to be. With his new 22nd century chemistry set, he sent his sister off to Alpha Centauri and back, to see if her boyfriend could wait. At the speed of light it took four years each way, eight for the round trip. Eight years the poor guy would have to wait. He waited patiently. He had no choice.

The boyfriend would go to their rendezvous spot every night till she returned. He was like a Shakespeare character in love. Well, he <u>was</u> in love. And it was a slow, arduous, painful process, waiting there for her all those long years when they could have been . . . well . . . doing things together. His sweetheart was worth waiting for, but still he felt like wringing her little brother's neck.

47

He thought that after eight years she would be a thirty-two-year-old woman with a middle-age sagging face and figure, and that he might have trouble recognizing her, but he knew he would love her anyway. Imagine his surprise and his joy when upon her return he saw that she had aged only eight months because of the time warp. He would still have a young bride. Now he would be the older one, an older man with a younger wife. Let his friends accuse him of robbing the cradle -- he didn't care.

But he couldn't get over the nagging thought that her nasty little brother had made him lose eight delicious years of togetherness with his love.

So he bought a bigger chemistry set for himself, and sent the little rapscallion off to Antares./1

THE END

/1 Antares, the brightest star in the constellation Scorpio, is some 600 light years distant from the solar system.

Hate Crime

Jacob Heller and Michael Dickens were about the same age and played together growing up. They lived outside of Oakview, a town of about 2,000 people in central Alabama.

They didn't know anything about racism, and didn't pay any attention to people's racial differences until they were ten years old and had to start going to school. They knew they were different from each other, and also different from some other kids, but it didn't bother them much. Jacob, or Jake as he was sometimes called, would tell Mike that his skin was dirty and that he should scrub the dirt off. Mike said Jake didn't have any skin, and that's why the sand gnats were always biting him. Sand gnats didn't bother Michael much; years of evolution in mosquito-infested African jungles had seen to that.

Modern studies suggest that it is not the type of skin one has, so much as the type of blood, that attracts mosquitoes and flies and gnats. These bugs seem to prefer common blood, like O-Positive (Jacob) and didn't like unusual types, like A-Negative (Michael), although of course the boys didn't know that that was the reason. As far as the bugs knew, there was no accounting for tastes, or as Gaius Julius Caesar would have put it, *de gustibus non est disputandum.*

Jacob's father liked to hunt and fish, and shoot tin cans for target practice with his old Mossberg single-shot bolt-action 0.22 rifle, so Jacob wanted to do that too. Of course

49

he was too young at first, but he did get a BB gun when he was eight. Jacob loved it and would spend hours shooting at tin cans and bottles and even acorns. He could hit an acorn about half the time at twenty feet -- he was that good.

The boys learned about race and racism in school in the sixties, when the popularity of polemical racial discussions and controversial arguments was sweeping across the country. Everybody had to choose a side; either you believed there were differences between the races, and that meant you were racist, or, if you were not racist, you believed that there was no difference between the races.

The two boys both liked football, and played on the high-school team. The coach made Jacob a quarterback because he seemed to be better at making quick decisions, and made Michael a defensive safety because he was tall and fast and had longer arms so he could block enemy passes.

But it was the quarterback who got the most admiration and acclaim. Michael then told the coach he wanted to be a quarterback too. "Yeah, I know," replied the coach. "Everybody wants to be quarterback. But I need you as safety. That's just as hard as being a quarterback, and just as important." At least that's what the coach told Michael. So Michael stayed there as defensive safety, like Deion Sanders, and it worked out fine.

About that time Jacob's father gave him a real gun, a 0.22 pistol, for his sixteenth birthday: a target pistol that had been made in Spain that his father won in a poker game. Perfect for Jacob. It would take three kinds of 0.22 cartridges: shorts, regulars, and longs, but not "long-rifle."

Jacob had to show it to Michael the first chance he got. It was the very next day. "Lemme see, lemme see," said Michael, who didn't know much about guns. The gun went off and shot Michael in the head, in the temple just in front of his ear.

The polarized racial communities, one pro-Black and the other pro-white, seized upon Michael's death as an ideal battlefield to attack each other with all sorts of accusations, asseverations, and vituperations, few of them well founded, many of them completely imaginary and fanciful. The case went to court. There was talk of bringing murder charges against Jacob, or should it just be manslaughter? Or was it an accident? Or had Jacob believed his position as football quarterback was threatened? The possibilities, and the fire and fury, and the obloquies and vituperations, flew back and forth in profusion. Then it was called a hate crime.

A hate crime is one that is much worse than its results. The idea of a hate crime is that the severity and nature of the thoughts leading a person to commit a crime are as important as, or even more important than, the crime itself. If you shoot a person for fun, or shoot a person that you love, that is naughty and you shouldn't have shot him. Too bad he is dead. But if you shoot a person who belongs to a group that you hate, that is much worse. You shouldn't have hated them. Hating *and* shooting is very, VERY naughty, twice as naughty as merely shooting someone for fun or for target practice. So your punishment must be double. Twenty years instead of ten for hating and shooting at the same time, both together. You should be hanged twice instead of once if you kill someone and hate him too. As Jacqueline Susann said, ONCE IS NOT ENOUGH.

51

Not everybody nor all societies view a so-called hate crime as worse than a non-hate crime that has the same result. It's the results that matter. If you shoot someone and put him in the hospital, it may be a good while before the nature of your crime can be ascertained. If he dies from his wounds a month later, we turn the calendar back and specify that your crime was murder. If he lives on in spite of the wound, your crime is much less severe, although the difference may depend upon the efficiency of the hospital staff or the skill of a surgeon, not upon the level of your hate for the victim or your accuracy with a firearm.

Most of us would agree that it is not nice to hate someone, but the law cannot tell you whom you may like or dislike. There is no law that says you cannot hate another person, if that's what you want to do. But the Law can tell you that you cannot injure other people, whether you love them or hate them. Nor may you kill them, regardless of whether you hate them or love them, or both.

How do you measure hate anyway? Not by the nature of a killing; some of the most gruesome murders involved loved ones. Identifying and proving premeditation is hard enough, and, for that matter, why is a premeditated murder considered more heinous than a spontaneous one? If I were to be murdered, I would be more afraid of the spontaneous murderer or a crazy man. If my wife or someone else I loved had killed me with premeditation, I might have seen it coming, but an impulsive spontaneous murder would have been harder to anticipate, and hence harder to avoid.

About that time, there was another hate crime in the news. It seems that a couple of street gangs had gotten into an altercation or a tussle, and it must have been pretty serious, for the switch-blade knives came out, and there was some cutting. Apparently, most of the cutting was done by one Black boy and one white boy, named Luther Cheever and Marco Desmond, respectively. Not only doing the cutting, but also getting cut.

As far as any blame for who started it, or whose fault it was, the evidence was inconclusive. The fault and the blame could have been spread further about to many others in both gangs. And that's about where the parallel ended. The two were cut up, but not equally. Some people may believe that, in a knife fight between a white boy and a Black boy, the Black boy will usually win, but that was not the case here. Marco got his knife in pretty deep and hit something in there that must have been rather vital. They both were taken to the hospital, Marco with superficial cuts, Luther facing surgery, with a serious internal wound, life threatening. Marco was discharged the next day, but Luther stayed on, in intensive care.

And the days and weeks of Luther's intensive-care hospitalization dragged on with neither his restoration nor his expiration clearly in the offing; the tension seemed endless. He was on the verge of death but he would not die. The public opinion polls were split about fifty-fifty. The bookies were taking bets: even odds. When Marco was well enough to go to jail, he was charged with a racist-inspired hate crime: attempted murder of a Black person. Because it was a hate crime, he would be tried as an adult.

The American newspapers and television anchormen were fascinated by the case. Americans love murders and other crimes of violence.

53

There was wild conjecture as to what punishment Marco would face if Luther died, as appeared likely. On the other hand, Marco found himself in the unusual position of praying for the health of someone he didn't like, and whom he was accused of hating, although he knew him only as a member of the other gang. Lawyers and law-school students discussed and argued the interesting question of what the penalty should be for a crime when its ultimate results were not yet known -- that is, had not yet taken place. Is it the deed (stabbing) that is the crime, or the effect of the deed (death or disfiguration) that is the crime? Which would be the more serious crime, shooting at someone with intent to kill but missing him, or shooting in the direction of someone with intent only to scare him but actually killing him? An interesting question.

* * * * *

The prosecuting attorney couldn't wait forever to learn whether Luther was going to die. He wanted to get on with it, and drew up charges of the State versus Marc Desmond for the hate crime of attempted murder of a Black man by a white man.

Now for most of the lifetime of this DA, the courts and public opinion had leaned toward the age-old prejudice of favoring the side of the white person involved in a white-Black altercation. By now, however, the pendulum had finally begun to swing the other way, and past prejudicial decisions were beginning to be "compensated" for by objective judgements and even occasional leanings toward the side of the Black person involved. In this particular case, the prosecuting DA himself was Black, and it looked as though no holds would be barred in the efforts to nail Desmond with all possible severity for this heinous hate crime. It appeared that Marco Desmond could get a sentence of 20 years if convicted of the hate crime of attempted murder, whereas if it were not a hate crime the sentence might have been only five years, for ordinary "attempted homicide without malice or premeditation."

Marco at this point needed a stroke of good luck. And as luck would have it, that's what he got.

The court appointed a public defender to serve as Marco's lawyer, a young eager beaver fresh out of law school and newly admitted to the bar, named Kurt Heiser. This would be Kurt's first big court case, his first attempted murder case anyway. Furthermore, it's racist overtones had brought the affair to front-page news across the state and indeed across the nation. Young Heiser needed to show his stuff on this case; his career depended on it.

It was clear that Desmond had severely wounded Cheever, and because the one was white and the other was Black, it was obviously a hate crime. "Not so fast," said Heiser to himself. A lot of "Blacks" have only 15% or 20% black blood in them. "Maybe I can get the court to acknowledge that Cheever was more white than black, and vitiate their racist-based hate crime accusation that way."

However, after some serious pondering, he realized that that wouldn't wash. The legal system and the entire nation had too deeply accepted the fact that a drop of black blood is all it takes to make a man Black. So he had to think some more.

It so happened that DNA testing to help determine people's ancestry was just getting popular in those days. Some Italians -- maybe not many -- had an occasional ancestor from Africa, many years ago, when Italy was involved in Abyssinia and other places in Africa. "I wonder if possibly . . ."

* * * * *

Eureka! The tests showed that Marco had approximately 1/64 black Ethiopian blood in his veins. That would make him a *sangmelee,* as they used to say in Haiti. He was Black! He had only been "passing" for white! You can't charge a Black man for a racist hate crime if it's Black against Black! Blacks can't hate Blacks!

And so he got Marco off with only five years in a moderate security prison. As far as Marco knows, the man he was accused of trying to kill is still in the hospital.

* * * * *

But back to our original case: you will remember that Jake, a white boy, and his friend Mike, a Black boy, were playing with a 0.22 pistol when it went off and shot Mike in the temple. Because, in America, racism is always a popular attraction in legal cases, Jake was charged with a hate crime -- attempted murder. The charged was modified to hate-based *murder* ten days later, when Jake died in the hospital. "I didn't hate him! I didn't! He was my friend," cried Jake, who was being held under house arrest until a date could be set for a preliminary hearing. "And I didn't shoot him; it was an accident! I swear! He was my friend!"

56

But the case was too valuable for the prosecuting District Attorney to ease up -- his reputation depended on his win/loss ratio. He needed this win, and pursued it doggedly, especially after Mike died and the charge was changed to murder -- murder exacerbated by racist hate.

However, the case never got to court -- Jake saw to that. As soon as he learned that Mike had died, he shot himself, also in the temple, with the same 0.22 pistol.

And this time death was almost immediate.

THE END

Poor Little Thing

Maia was born in a suburb of Lisbon. Lisbon is a beautiful, bustling city with many fancy restaurants and theaters, lovely parks, churches, and museums, but some parts of its suburbs, such as Amadora to the north of the City, are not so beautiful. There is a suburb of Amadora called Cova da Moura, which is less beautiful than the rest of Amadora. In fact it is a very poor area that many people would call a slum, and that's where Maia was born and where she has lived all her life.

Cova da Moura, or simply Moura, is well known for its poverty and for the interesting architecture of some of its old run-down buildings and shacks on the hillside above Lisbon. Moura has been likened to the poor *favelas* on the slopes surrounding Rio de Janiero. In recent years, parts of Amadora and Moura have become something of an attraction for fancy tourists who "have seen everything" and are now "going slumming." Small tour groups come to Moura on day trips from the big Lisbon hotels just to look and take photographs showing "how the other half lives." (Day trips only; to add to the mystique, they say nighttime trips would be too dangerous.)

Amadora used to be something of a linen center, before the booming mechanization of weaving and lace-making in Belgium and Ireland drove the handworkers almost completely out of business. Jobs in Moura now go mostly to laborers and cleaners, but nevertheless, there are still a

59

few families in Moura, women that is, that continue to eke out a living selling lovely hand-woven linen products such as table cloths and bedspreads. Maia's mother and elder sister, Costança, had been able to sell their toilsome hand work at meager prices to some of the tourists who come on adventure walks through their area.

When Maia's grandmother was alive, she taught Maia how to crochet, and Maia loved it. Sadly, when Maia was only eight years old, her grandmother died, but Maia by then felt she knew enough about crocheting to do it on her own. She applied herself to the work assiduously and completed a set of twelve doilies and place mats. They were just the way Grandma would have made them, and Maia was very proud. One bright Saturday morning in spring she took her wares to one of the parks in the center of Moura. The central park, or "praça," bore but a vestige of its former elegance, and now was little more than a vacant lot with a few palm trees and cedars and native shrubs growing fallow along the slope of the hill, but it was a "destination" for occasional tourist groups with their cameras, walking through the area.

Maia spread her wares out in the shade of a cedar tree, carefully arranging them in an attractive pattern that would catch the eye of any prospective customer. Then she had to wait. She waited all morning and half the afternoon, and although several groups of well-dressed foreigners came strolling by under the watchful eye of a professional guide from an agency like Cook's Tours, none stopped to buy. Maia couldn't understand it. She knew her work was beautiful, done by hand in the old traditional manner.

Finally an elderly gentleman stopped and looked at the girl. Maybe he will buy something, thought Maia, her hopes now aroused. "How old are you?" He asked. Maia told him, but she would rather have talked about her linens. "My grandmother taught me how to crochet," she explained. "That's the way people used to make things, a long time ago. See?" she said holding up an attractive pair of doilies. "Would you like to buy some?" she asked hopefully.

The man probably did not mean to sound cruel when he truthfully said, "I have no use for such things," but to little Maia it sounded as though he did not like her work. Then the man reached into his pocket and said, "Here, take this," and gave her forty dollars.

Maia replied, "Oh, thank you; which ones would you like?"

But the man just shook his head and simply said, "That's all right," turned, and was on his way.

"But Sir!" said Maia. By then the man did not hear her.

After a while, with no more luck, Maia went on home and gave her mother the money. Her mother was delighted, but by then Maia was crying profusely.

"Why are you crying my dear? Look at all the money you made selling doilies."

"I didn't make any money," she sobbed. "I didn't sell any; he didn't like them. He . . . he gave me the money for

. . . for pity. 'You poor little girl,' he said to me. He didn't buy and I didn't sell," she muttered between her tears. "He didn't buy any of my work. Nothing. Nobody did. I didn't sell anything at all," she sobbed.

THE END

In a Jam

We were in a jam. I could tell. No doubt about it. How we got there might need some explanation.

To begin with, it was all Leonardo's fault. Well, it was our fault too, but if it hadn't been for Leonardo, it never would have happened. I mean Leonardo da Vinci, not Leonardo di Caprio. Caprio might have been the actor's last name, but Vinci just happened to be the place were the other Leonardo was born. A lot of people back in the olden days didn't really have a last name. You see, some of them weren't always sure who their father was, so they just used the name of their town or village as sort of a last name. Vinci is a little village in the Tuscan hills near Florence, so Leonardo called himself Leonardo da Vinci, just like Leonardo di Caprio could have called himself Leonardo di Los Angeles, but he didn't. Leonardo thought Leonardo da Vinci had a nice euphonious ring to it that would sound good in the history books, and, as it turned out, he was right, for it's one of the most famous names you will see anywhere; all the history books say so.

That Leonardo, when he wasn't painting, liked to invent things, and besides army tanks and helicopters, he was the one who invented locks, like locks in canals, so boats could go up and down between waters of different levels, from rivers and lakes to oceans and bays, without all the water from one level running down into the water of the lower level, as it would have done before Leonardo came along.

Before Leonardo, all they had was single harbor gates to control the water level, like they still have today at St. Katherine Dock in London by the Tower Bridge, and in Texas City, and in New Bedford. At St. Katherine Dock the gate is open for only about two hours before and after high tide on the Thames and then remains closed for ten or eleven hours to hold the water in and keep the boats afloat in the little harbor. The level of the Thames River in that area drops fifteen or twenty feet at low tide, so, without the watergate, at low tide all the boats in the dock would be hard aground. The gates at Texas City and New Bedford are used primarily to protect against occasional storm surges accompanying unusually high tides.

But Leonardo's invention of the canal lock, comprising two gates with water trapped between, allows the water and boats in the lock to go up or down, bringing navigation to rivers and lakes which previously were inaccessible to boats, except by portage, and good only for local traffic, plus swimming and sunbathing perhaps.

Following Leonardo's designs, locks were used for many decades in Italy's Po River Valley and elsewhere, and subsequently in many other parts of the civilized world, from Amsterdam, to Erie, to Panama.

Right away the installation and use of locks opened up many more little canals and waterways for small boats and barges moving about over longer distances, from one part of the country to another, or from rivers and lakes to the ocean. There were already canals around places like Venice and Amsterdam and Bruges, but with locks, canal use soon extended throughout the Po River Valley, most of the Netherlands, Norfolk and East Anglia, and even the Garonne-Rhone area of southern France. With three locks along the Willebroek Canal, Brussels gained easy access by water to Antwerp and the sea. In due course it became possible for small boats and barges to go all the way from Brussels to Paris by canals, from London to Manchester, from Paris to Avignon, and indeed from Bordeaux and the Bay of Biscay to Toulouse and the Mediterranean Sea, as well as from the upper regions of the Rhine and its tributary the Main in Germany through Bamberg to the Blue Danube and on to the Black Sea. These waterways and their locks make for profitable commercial traffic and popular cruising grounds for tourists and vacationers to this day.

In due course, larger canals with massive locks were built, connecting bodies of water of different elevations, such as the Sault Ste Marie Canal and the Welland Canal, as well as crossing land barriers between seas, such as the Kiel Canal, the North Sea Canal between Amsterdam and IJmuiden, or the Atlantic-Pacific canal in Panama with its six locks between oceans.

My family and I have always loved boats and sailing, especially small sailboats and big oceans. We have sailed our boat through many of the canals and locks mentioned above, and in due course it became time for us to do the Panama Canal.

* * * * *

Now compared to most of the canals and locks we were familiar with, the Panama Canal locks were enormous, 110 feet wide and several hundred feet long. Some small canals of Europe and England limit the beam of allowable vessels to fourteen feet or less. On the other hand, many canals of Europe with great systems of locks for ocean-going vessels, for instance the Kiel Canal, the North Sea Canal, and Willemstad in the Dordrecht waterway now have redundant parallel sets of locks for separate use of large vessels and tiny boats. Use of a set of small locks for small boats is both a safety measure and a means of conserving water, which of course is lost with the passage of every vessel.

The Panama Canal had no such offering of separate parallel locks for smaller vessels. Sometimes the passage through the canal was delayed until a number of small boats had gathered and were brought into the locks together, a convenience and a water-saving practice.

Occasionally a moderately large vessel transiting the Panama Canal would leave enough room in the end of the lock to allow one or two small boats to sneak in as well. In this case the small boats were logically required to wait and enter the lock after the large vessel had done so, and, if possible, exit first, because of the violent disruptive currents caused by any movement of the large vessel.

At that time I owned a beautiful miniature ocean-going yacht, a 25-foot sloop of the "tetranora" design, built by David Cheverton in Cowes, made of carvel-strip mahogany with a full cast-iron keel, drawing about four feet.

My wife and daughter and I have sailed in many places in Europe and North America, in oceans and bays, and various canals, through tiny locks and great ones.

Last year it came time for us to test the Panama Canal, for that was a major part of our plan to sail from our place in North Carolina to visit my cousins in San Francisco on the Bay. We would spend most of the summer on the voyage, about six or eight weeks. The transit of the Panama Canal would be an important and exciting part of our trip.

An old school friend of mind, Plimpton Farmwell, that I had sailed with once on the Chesapeake Bay, heard of our plans and asked to join us for our transit of the Canal. Sure, why not, I said. The boat had four berths and, as there were only three of us, we did occasionally take another family member or a friend along for a ride.

Plimpton was not a seasoned sailor, but had been out on the water a couple of times and could hold a line or a sheet if you showed him which way to pull it.

He flew in to Panama the day after we got there on the boat. We had anchored in the "flats" off the Panama Canal Yacht Club in Cristobal for customs and a day or two of relaxation and resupply. Then Plimpton came across from the airport on the little train that runs periodically over the fifty miles from Panama City on the Pacific to the Atlantic side. We all had a nice dinner together at the fine old Washington Hotel in Colon. It was a pleasure to enjoy someone else's cooking for a change, and to feel *terra firma* under our feet after some weeks at sea. We then had two more days for catching up on some shipboard maintenance and a bit of local sightseeing before we set out one bright Tuesday morning for our transit of the Canal. We planned to take it easy -- two days for the passage, with overnight anchoring in a cove on the great Gatun Lake.

67

Tuesday all went well. Plimpton was actually a help. He was trim and strong, and I showed him how to hold a dock line and adjust it as we went up with the rising water in the Gatun locks. We were with about half a dozen other small boats of various sizes making the passage. We went through the three sets of locks with no trouble, taking care to fend off our boat from the fierce granite walls of that man-made canyon, as the incoming water poured in and swirled about, raising our boat almost thirty feet each time, in three stages, over eighty feet in all.

The cruise across Gatun Lake that afternoon was spectacular. We saw decaying skeletons of giant mahogany trees that had been swamped by the rising waters of this new artificial lake over a hundred years ago. We saw former hilltops that were now tropical islands, like Barro Colorado, which is now a Smithsonian Tropical Research station, devoted largely to the study of adaptations and evolution of new species of bugs and insects etc. in sudden isolation from their continental relatives, having been cut off and isolated by the creation of the lake.

Late Wednesday morning we saw an enormous cruise ship -- *Caribbean Princess,* I think she was called -- sweep past us as we were leaving Gatun Lake heading southeast/1 toward Miraflores ("see the pretty flowers"). Before Miraflores there is only one lock, Pedro Miguel, our first step down toward the Pacific, but a drop of about thirty feet. The rise and fall in the locks of the Panama Canal was

---

/1 Because of a curious geographic twist, the south-eastern end of the Panama Canal is on the Pacific.

considerably greater than anything we had ever experienced before -- greater than that of the great locks we had known in Kiel and Dordrecht/Willemstad.

As we approached Pedro Miguel we saw that the big cruise ship had gone on ahead and was just entering the lock. There was plenty of space behind her in the lock, and as soon as the ship had stopped, a bull horn instructed us to enter on the starboard side. The big ship itself did not tie up directly, but was held in place by lines running ashore to four heavy rail cars called mules. The tension in these lines was controlled automatically and adjusted accordingly as the water level rose or fell. In our small boat we were given shore lines to hold and adjust by hand as necessary. Plimpton took the line that had been thrown onto our foredeck. I took the aft line. We put out our fenders to protect our topsides from the rough granite walls, and held our lines. We were ready for the descent -- ready for the water level to drop.

But nobody else seemed ready. Some of the passengers on the cruise ship had gathered on the fantail to watch the proceedings, and apparently to watch us. As I said, we did have a pretty little boat. I felt as though I were playing the part of a nude ephebus on the stage of a rerun of "Oh, Calcutta!" but that was little compared to the excitement that was soon to come.

I don't know why it took so long for the canal operators to close the lock gate behind us and start the process of lowering us down to the next level so we could be on our way. Maybe they were waiting for another vessel. There was still enough room in the lock for another ship if it were not too big. The lock was over 1000 feet long.

Plimpton must have thought so too, as I was soon to learn, for he apparently got tired of holding the bow line and tied it to the main cleat on the foredeck, the one we usually use for securing the anchor rode when at anchor.

Meanwhile the great gate did close, silently, and then, rather suddenly, and with little warning, the water level started rapidly dropping. I had to take a half turn of my stern line about a cleat, as the stern seemed to be going down faster than the bow.

"Ease off a little faster there on the bow line," I called to Plimpton. I temporarily had to cleat my own line to try to keep the boat more or less on an even keel, so to speak. No response.

"Ease off there!" I repeated, this time as forcefully as I could. By then our stern was about three feet lower than the bow: we were pitched up at an angle of at least 20 degrees.

"Plimpton!" I screamed. "What are you doing?

"I . . . I can't," he babbled, beginning to sound slightly desperate. "It's stuck."

"Stuck . . . ? Uncleat it and ease it off!" I bellowed.

The water continued to drop. Faster now. I had to keep my line cleated to hold the boat from taking an even steeper angle.

I could sense impending difficulties.

70

I called out to one of the mule-drivers on the quayside, saying to stop the outflow of water until we could get squared away. Perhaps he couldn't hear me because of the noise of the rushing water, a giant toilet bowl, gurgling down, down. I tried to signal him to put the cork back in the drain hole to stop the outflow, but apparently my gesture was ambiguous and he misunderstood it, for he flipped me an unambiguously unkind and impolite gesture in return.

By then my sweet little wife and daughter had come out of the companionway and asked, "What's going on? Why are you tipping the boat this way?"

I only had time to say, "Watch this cleat." I gave them the bitter end of the stern line and climbed up as quickly as I could to the foredeck. I grabbed the shore line from Plimpton, but no use. He had cleated it upside down, with the end of the line coming out by the bottom of the cleat. All tension on the top now, on the shore line, hard as nails, impossible to pay out or loosen it at all.

By then our boat was out of the water completely, hanging crazily against the wall, held by two shore lines, bow and stern, unable to zig or to zag, The water had dropped six feet and had another 24 feet to go. Just as I was thinking up the most suitable swear word to express my concern and the severity of the situation, an unnecessarily loud bull horn came blasting through my eardrums.

"Ahoy! Ahoy sailboat, starboard side Pedro Miguel Lock Number One, HEAR THIS!" I don't know why he called it

71

Lock Number One;   it's the only lock there is, there at Pedro Miguel.

"You there, Sailboat! Stop what you are doing! Stop it immediately! You are creating a disturbance! You are not allowed to stay tied to the quay when the water is descending. Your behavior is not in accordance with Canal regulations, and you must stop it! Stop it immediately, do you hear? Immediately! This is an order under the authority of his Excellency Harold Q. Parfitt, Governor of the Canal Zone and President of the Panama Canal Company. Now stop it!"

By then the stern of the *Caribbean Princess* was so loaded with curious onlookers that the great vessel had taken on a bow-up angle of its own of at least one and a half degrees. I tried to smile for the benefit of the crowd, but it was difficult.

The best I could do was to face the direction of the bull horn and tell them, as loudly and as clearly as I could under the circumstances, "We're having . . . problems." In fact, we were in a jam.

I knew we were in a jam.

I could tell.

THE END

Sexual Abuse

I am not bad looking, if I do say so myself. I have all my teeth and a nice smile, wavy blonde hair, smooth skin and not much hair on my legs. And I have a pretty good build according to some of my friends' friends. But good looks can be both an asset and a liability. They will generally help in social situations as well as job situations. They may help your career but may also help to get you into trouble. I'll show you what I mean.

My name is Brandon Pierson, although some people want to call me Brandy, a name I dislike intensely. In the first place I am a tea-totaler, and I don't even drink wine, let alone the hard stuff. An occasional beer perhaps, after a golf game, but that's it. And I hate names like Brandy, and Bobby or Bobbie, and Jamie, and Prescott -- names like that, which could be either girls' names or boys' names.

I am single, unmarried, no children, and I have my own apartment in a little town, or bedroom community, just 25 miles from the Big City where I work. Sometimes I chuckle to myself when I hear the term "bedroom community," because I know that we have a lot of activities going on all the time in many bedrooms in our area; however, so far, I have always been able to steer clear of most of such activities and the problems that often accompany or soon follow them.

I got the idea for this scheme just the other day, when I was re-reading a clipping I had cut out of the paper several months ago, in September 2016. It read as follows:

The parent company of Fox News, Twentieth Century Fox Corporation, will reportedly pay 20 million dollars to settle a lawsuit brought by former TV anchor Gretchen Carlson, who said Roger Allen sexually harassed her when he was chairman of the network -- and provided solid evidence. Two other women have allegedly settled similar lawsuits and at least one other is pending. The Corporation issued an apology in which it acknowledged that "Gretchen was not treated with the respect and dignity that she and all of our colleagues deserve."

"Wow! Twenty million dollars! That's a lot of money," I thought, as the wheels in the analytic corner of my brain started wildly spinning about. "Gee, twenty million at three per cent would yield, let's see -- $600,000 per year, or about $1,600 a day. I could live on half of that, even with my high-class tastes."

I have been working in the City for five years now, first as Cashier and then as Assistant Manager of an up-scale shoe store in a big shopping mall. I like my job all right; the pay and the working conditions are adequate, although I certainly am not getting rich. But the news clipping gave me an idea.

The truth is that I too have been sexually molested on various occasions. I never complained or said anything about it, assuming it just came with the job.

74

It was something you just put up with, unless you are one of those people who can simply relax and enjoy it, or at least pretend to enjoy it. Frankly, I didn't always enjoy it -- not always anyway -- and sometimes didn't even like to pretend, although I never made a big issue of it. For one thing, I didn't want to jeopardize my job. But if Gretchen Carlson could get twenty million . . .

Actually, I didn't really mind it -- sexual attentions in inappropriate places, shall we say. In fact, I rather liked the idea of knowing I was attractive enough to have my boss, the manager, and sometimes a few others, want to caress my neck and shoulders while casually walking past my desk, or even doing more things with me when I was called into the manager's office "to discuss important business matters." But anyway, like I said, I didn't always mind it. I simply relaxed and tried to enjoy. But on reading this article about Gretchen Carlson, I realized I had a golden opportunity right in front of me. I didn't need 20 million; one quarter of that, or even one tenth, would have been sufficient. At that point I began to record on a yellow pad the number of occasions on which I was summoned to the manager's office for purposes outside of regular store business. I would sometimes call attention to what was going on by mentioning to my colleagues that "the manager wants to see me," or "I have to go to the manager's office," so I would have witnesses when I needed them.

With my mind made up and my plans comfortably developing before me, I went to a law firm that had advertised on TV that they loved cases of sexual harassment. I didn't really feel that I had been harassed, and certainly not beaten or abused. The fact is that I had often enjoyed my tête-a-têtes with the manager, but I had to build up a story. Certainly, however, like Gretchen Carlson, I had not been "treated with respect and dignity." That much was pure truth. My lawyer said it was clearly a case of sexual harassment and that we should forcefully proceed along those lines.

"Five million will be enough," I told her. I'm not a greedy person, and I wanted to be fair about this. Besides, if that Carson dame from the television company could get twenty million, my people should be glad to get off easy at five million. She agreed, and took the case on the understanding of a fee equal to 20% of a favorable judgement, that is, one million for her and four million for me if we won. Four million should be enough for me to live on, at least for the rest of my life, if I spent it carefully and thriftily, and didn't live too long. After all, my investment in the case had been minimal, which is to say nothing at all, so anything I was awarded would mathematically represent an infinite percentage gain over my original investment.

We were all set to go. She filed the papers and after a few days we were given a court date for the middle of the following month. It all proceeded as planned.

Up to a point.

* * * * *

The judge reviewed the briefs the lawyers had prepared, examined the supporting documents, and had the bailiff call the court to order.

"This seems to be a clear case of sexual harassment," declared the judge. "I am sick and tired of seeing this epidemic of sexual harassment and abuse spreading through every nook and cranny across the United States. I don't know what has happened to our morality and family values, and our sense of equality of the sexes. Now, I would like to ask the plaintiff some questions . . . Where is the plaintiff?"

I was already standing up. "I am the plaintiff, your Honor."

"No, I mean the plaintiff in this sexual harassment case."

"I am the plaintiff in this sexual harassment case, your Honor."

"You are . . . ? State your name, please."

"My name is Brandon Pierson," your Honor. "Some people, including the defendant, THE POINTED SHOE COMPANY, call me Brandy, but I don't like that name very much and would rather just be called Brandon."

"But you're a man!"

"Yes, your Honor. I was named for my maternal grandfather, Brandon Bradford. He was a man too."

"Young man, don't you be making fun of this court!"

"Yes, your Honor . . . I mean, NO your Honor. I wouldn't do that."

77

"And you say you were ordered to go to the manager's office, and then you were sexually molested there?"

"Yes, your Honor. And furthermore I wasn't treated with respect and dignity."

"Was the manager a man or a woman?"

"Yes, your Honor . . . I mean she was a woman. In fact, she was quite a woman, your Honor, I'll say that for her. But she was my manager, you know? You know what I mean, your Honor?"

"I think I am beginning to get the picture. And the picture I am getting is not leaning in your favor, young man. You have deceived the court by the presentation in your brief in which you consciously refrain from revealing the gender of the plaintiff, and indeed imply that the plaintiff was a woman, or could have been."

"There was no such inference implied or intended, your Honor. I am only seeking equal treatment before the law, regarding race, creed, and gender equality, your Honor."

"You know perfectly well what I mean. You are trying to make a mockery of this court, and if you don't cease and desist I will hold you in contempt. You are a man and your charges of sexual harassment are ridiculous."

". . . But, your Honor . . ."

"Case dismissed."

THE ORIGINAL END

78

Epilogue

I was disappointed, but not too surprised, to tell the truth. I knew the idea of gender equality in America at this stage was still a mythical chimera.

On the way out of the courtroom, my lawyer gave me a pat on the back and said, "Buck up, old boy. We are not done yet. We'll file a suit against the State for violation of your civil rights, and for violation of the Civil Rights Amendment. In legal matters, men now have a perfect right to be treated just like people. I mean like other people, like women. Some men have even won child-custody cases. We have a watertight case. Even the judge said you are a man. We'll get a copy of today's transcript and submit it with a new plea, alleging our equal rights were infringed upon and violated."

"All right," I said, "we've come this far; no point in quitting now." My lawyer still sounded very optimistic, and I was thinking it certainly would be worth the effort to take one more stab at winning that five million dollars. Well, four million anyway.

That's when my lawyer said, "We'll shoot for ten million. Sometimes you are more likely to win a case if you ask for a lot, like that Carson dame on TV did. You ever hear of her?"

THE FINAL END

Cold Turkey

Some people think that, if someone is good in one thing, he must be good in anything, or that if he knows a lot about something, he knows a lot about everything. I remember reading a book by Albert Einstein no less, entitled IDEAS AND OPINIONS. I thought it was mostly vapid platitudes, nothing esoteric as one might expect, but indeed, on the contrary, rather commonplace, even <u>exoteric</u>. Stuff I thought almost anyone could have written.

Our family doctor, Ives Taggart, is that way too. He wants to tell you what to do even in matters that don't have very much to do with health, like taste in food.

For instance, I have a friend on a farm who has his own smokehouse and smokes his own bacon and ham. Sometimes he lets me smoke turkey there too. And smoked turkey is really good for picnics on the beach, especially when eaten cold in sandwiches either with cheese or with lettuce and tomato and lots of mustard.

I'm sixty-six years old, and I've never had any particular problems with my health since I had my tonsils out, but I get an annual check-up every year anyway. This year Dr. Ives told me, rather forcefully, I thought, that I should "quit smoking cold turkey."

I don't know where Dr. Taggart gets his ideas and opinions from. He may be a good doctor, but he doesn't know what he is talking about when it comes to turkey sandwiches.

THE END

Soft Life

A lot of people, kids mostly, grow up in the inner-city slums of various metropolitan centers all over the world, including the Atlantic seaboard and New England coast of the United States, and many other places. As a rule, it seems the bigger the city, the bigger the slums. And the richer the rich, the poorer the poor And the softer the good life, the harsher the not-so-good life.

When he was a little kid, all Felix knew was misery. If he thought at all, he thought that it was just the way things were. You get punched or whipped for taking an extra cookie. Your parents (or parent) and older brothers and sisters scream at you for no reason at all, because that's all they know how to do. They scream and fight with each other too.

Felix Fenton and his family of eight lived in a tenement house with three other big families. Nobody seemed to like anybody else, and there was always screaming and yelling and fighting going on.

When Felix was old enough to go to school, it was a bit of a relief for him to get out of the house and the noise and chaos and squabblings and beatings.

But there were disruptions and fights in school too, and Felix wasn't really very happy in school either. He was a slow student; he got put back a grade a couple of times, so

83

he didn't start high school in the ninth grade until he was almost 17 years old./1

Felix didn't like high school much either, but stuck it out for a couple of years until he was past 18. But during those two years, Felix connected with a group of guys, some in school and some not, who called themselves "The Enforcers." They claimed it was not a "gang," but a "group." Gangs had a negative image, and were frowned upon by law-enforcement authorities, and were treated correspondingly harshly, just for being a "gang."

Felix never got any spending money to speak of from home. He learned how to snitch things from the K-Mart and the Rexall Drug Store, things that he could use or sell, a cigarette lighter, a pocket knife, a wrist watch, a couple of Parker pens. Mostly little things. Other people had these things; why shouldn't Felix have them too? All it took was money. But Felix didn't have any money. He had to steal. He had no choice.

Then he learned about drugs. Not just tasting them, or smoking them, but making money off them. Buying and selling. That's the way people make money, by buying and selling. Walmart doesn't make anything. They buy and sell. They buy low and sell high. Felix was learning about economics; on-the-job training, you might say.

/1 In the old days, if you flunked you had to redo the year. Probably not that way anymore; now it seems everyone goes on to the next grade level whether he needs to, or should, or not.

Felix could make a little money by buying drugs from older kids and selling them to younger kids in smaller packages but at a profit. It wasn't making him rich, but helped him get by. He didn't spend any more time in his home than he had to. His better home was the streets. He even slept in the streets sometimes if it wasn't too cold.

That went on for a few more miserable years. Felix was never happy, even when he had made a sale, for then other members of the gang were on his back to try to make him share. Make him share, but they never would share when it was their turn, the other way around.

His parents said he should "get out there and get a job," and make some money, but they silently knew he was making some money doing drugs, and made him contribute to the household expenses, "something for all the food and the clothes and everything we have bought for you over the years."

About that time, Felix heard about some crook who had figured out how to break into an ATM machine and had stolen over ten thousand dollars. "Wow," thought Felix. "That's better than swiping cigarette lighters."

So that gave him inspiration. He bought all the newspaper accounts of the incident, and even a radical tabloid that had a piece explaining how it might have been done. He had to get one of his group of "Persuaders" to read it to him because his reading skills were not too good, and there were several words in the article that he didn't know.

85

"I can do that," thought Felix. So he did.

At least he tried. He tried the ATM at a local bank about 3:30 one night, when things were relatively quiet. But just as he was about to get the front of the machine off, an alarm rang, and in no time there were two big watchmen with badges hauling him off by the elbows to jail.

He was tried and convicted of attempted grand larceny of a bank. As it was an unsuccessful endeavor, he was sentenced to one year in prison instead of five.

Now the good news is that, somehow, Felix's prison sentence got mixed up with the numerous cases of financial crimes of white-collar bankers and rich CEO's and politicians and the like, typically relating to defalcations involving fraudulent tax returns, money laundering, usury, falsification of accounts, illegal short sales, and currency exchange manipulations, as well as simple embezzlement./2 The perpetrators of these clean, non-violent, crimes are not viewed by our authorities as a great security threat to our society or to the Establishment. Accordingly, such non-violent criminals, including rich men, bankers, CEO's, and sometimes even government officials and politicians, who know people or have friends in important places, are typically incarcerated in facilities known as "minimal security correctional institutions." Often they do not even have enclosure walls or fences.

/2 Some people believe embezzlement is the same as theft. It is not, although it is related. See THE EMBEZZLER, in *Short Stories You'll Love*, by Daniel Hoyt Daniels, p 145.

One such penitentiary, known for its relatively soft prison life and pleasant conditions, is at Frostburg, Maryland, nestled in the rolling green foothills of the Appalachian Mountains. Apparently because the Fenton case involved a bank, and not a convenience store or a gas station, Felix was thrown in with the white-collar (also white-skinned) criminals, and sentenced to one year incarceration at Frostburg.

Well, let me tell you, this was better than anything Felix had. ever known. For the first time in his life he had regular meals and his own cot to sleep on. The work requirements involved modest exercise, mostly clean-up and yard work in the fresh air, which he actually liked, quite different from his polluted life in the inner City. The prison library had books for studying English and many other subjects. One of the other prisoners, who had been an English teacher on the outside and was finding life a bit boring on the inside, took an interest in Felix and helped him greatly improve his reading skills.

Felix never had it so good. His year went by all too fast.

* * * * *

Upon his release from prison, Felix went back to the street scene, the only place and the only life he had ever known outside of Frostburg.

He was miserable. All his old acquaintances were still there, still just as stupid, quarrelsome, mean, aggressive, and unfriendly as ever. His parents were now divorced, but neither of them would to have anything to do with this "ex-convict." He was on his own, on the street, once again.

The pleasant memory of Frostburg haunted him. "Oh, why didn't they give me ten years instead of only one? I wish I were back there," he thought. His thoughts ran on. "Maybe I could . . . " he wondered . . . "do something. But what?" Thereupon he went to his city library, with new confidence in his recently improved reading skills, to do some research on various crimes and their respective punishments.

His study showed that a very serious, but non-violent, crime was the death threat, particularly when directed against a Federal official, such as a US Senator, or a District Attorney, or perhaps a Federal Judge. You threaten his life with an anonymous note. You don't harm him, but the authorities track you down and give you a nice long sentence, maybe five or ten years, for the threat. Just right. Just what I am looking for! This street scene is not for me; it's for the birds.

So he did it.

He wrote the note in his own handwriting, such as it was. He wasn't trying to hide anything. He pretended in the note that he wanted to do the judge a favor, but hoped it would be viewed as a serious threat. The note was somewhat ambiguous, reading as follows:

TO JUDGE TERRY ENDIVE: DERE JUDGE, I JEST WANTED TO LET YOU KNOW THAT YOUR LIFE IS IN GRATE DANGER. THER ARE PEOPLE WHO ARE PLANING TO KILL YOU ONE OF THES DAYS SOON, SO WATCH OUT. YOUR FREIND, FELIX

Felix didn't give his last name or any other information --
no return address, of course. He didn't want them to think
that he was eager for them to catch him, but was smart
enough to realize that, as Felix, he was known to the cops
in the area, and that they wouldn't have too much trouble
finding him if they wanted to.

As Felix visualized the scenario, they would find him,
grill him for details and accomplices, make him confess to
the note, and give him a nice sentence of five or ten years
in Frostburg. His plan was perfect. All he had to do was
wait a few days -- maybe a week or two -- for them to
come and arrest him, and then he would be on his way.

But it didn't work out quite like that.

* * * * *

By chance, only three days after Felix mailed the fateful
letter, Judge Terrence (Terry) Endive was shot in the head
and killed getting out of his car at home, one evening after
work. Apparently there were some people in this world
that really hated Judge Endive, probably for severe
sentences that he had handed down from the bench. As the
TV news reported it, the unknown assassin or assassins had
apparently been waiting for the opportunity in a parked car
near the judge's residence.

Sometimes the police are slow to act. Not this time. The
very next morning they found Felix Fenton on one of his
usual street corners, trying to act nonchalant. (He had not
heard of the Judge's murder.)

Felix was duly arrested and charged with being an accomplice in a murder. "Maybe you didn't pull the trigger, but you were part of the plan, and that's the same thing. Everyone that's in cahoots in a murder is equally and fully guilty. But it would be nice of you anyway, to tell us who the others were."

Felix was, well, speechless. "I don't know anything about it," he stammered.

"Who are you trying to kid? We have your note right here, see?"

So Felix was tried and convicted of premeditated murder in the first degree. Circumstantial evidence, beyond a reasonable doubt. (The real culprits have never been apprehended, and the case has been closed.)

But Felix didn't get Frostburg this time, nor did he get the five or ten years he was hoping for. He got life imprisonment at Sing Sing, one of the most notorious, vile and abhorred, maximum security prisons anywhere. Miserable conditions. Not nice at all.

THE END

Her Best Offer

I don't pick up hitch-hikers much. Not anymore. I used to sometimes, particularly around our neighborhood, if the fellow seemed to be a local. I used to hitch-hike myself occasionally, for instance if we were coming home from school and waiting for a bus to take us from the city out to the suburbs. I once hitch-hiked all the way from Norfolk, Virginia to Chambersburg, Pennsylvania. But not anymore. Nowadays you hear about too many horrible things that can happen to hitch-hikers or to the people that pick hitch-hikers up. I have read that in Finland, and perhaps some other developed and civilized countries, they actually encourage something like hitch-hiking, but it is organized. The state checks people out and issues ID's and authorization cards to both hikers and drivers, with a supply of blank receipt forms to sign and exchange. The hiker pays the driver a small sum to help cover gasoline expenses, and the whole thing is recorded and official. Sounds complicated, but it's not. It works fine all around. We should adopt a system like that in our own country.

Between my house and my office in the city, I have about a 30-mile commute, mostly on a two-lane state highway. On my way home from work, last Thursday I believe it was, I saw a young girl by the side of the road who looked over her shoulder at me and sort of gestured with her right hand as I passed her. I couldn't tell if she had her thumb up in the standard hitch-hiking fashion, but she seemed to be asking for a ride. She can't be much of a threat, I thought;

maybe she does need a ride. So I slowed down and stopped the car, then backed up fifty yards or so.

The girl looked to be about thirteen years old, small and slim, wearing a button sweater and a skirt that was too long for her, like you often used to see poor country girls wearing. I was surprised to note that she wore bright red lipstick, as though she were a little child who had gotten into her mother's cosmetic box and was playing "dress up."

She came up to my car window, but didn't say anything. I asked her, "Where are you going? Do you want a ride?"

She hesitated, sort of looking me over to make sure I seemed all right, then politely said, "That wud be ver nahss uh few."

"Where are you going?"

"Ahm go'n' . . ." She paused . . . "Ahm go'n' tuh see mah gran-mudduh."

"Does your grandmother live around here?"

"It's jes down da road a piece, mebbie fi, six mile. I wuz gwina walk."

"Well, let me know when you want to get off."

"Okay." So she got in.

Then I asked, "Do you go to school?"

"I use to, but not much any mo'. Anyways it's sum-ma vacation now, so it don' make no dif'unce."

"How old are you?"

"Ah's sixteen, but Ah'l be sebn-teen befo' long." She looked more like thirteen to me, but I didn't pursue the matter. Women always lie about their age anyway.

We were quiet after that, as I wondered about the strange, unattached life this little waif must be leading. She obviously came from a poor family. Her skirt was made of cheap denim, probably homemade. Her cardigan had a patched elbow, but her shirt looked clean and her hair was combed and tidy. She was a pretty little thing, and I couldn't help feeling sorry for her.

After ten or fifteen minutes she broke the silence and said, "Iss de nes road, ri dova der." I turned off the highway onto the dirt road she had indicated. It didn't seem to be much of a road; it looked more like a turn-around spot. I stopped the car. There was nothing but some cornfields and some woods so far as I could see. No houses or farms in sight. "Where does your grandmother live?" I asked. "I don't see any houses or anything at all."

"Oh, tha's okay; Ah kin walk there from heah."

"I don't mind taking you there; I'm not in any hurry."

"Well, all ri . . . It's jes a mile er so."

So I drove slowly on down the dirt road, which wasn't much more that a narrow path in the woods by then, until another dirt path turned off to the right. "Iss here," she said.

I still couldn't see any sign of life or habitation; it was just cornfields and woods, mostly woods. "Ah'll gi tao chea."

Wait a minute," I said, thinking how sorry I was for this poor thing wandering about this way. "Let me give you this," as I pulled out my wallet and gave her a ten-dollar bill. Her eyes lit up. You would have thought she had never seen a ten-dollar bill before in her life. Maybe she hadn't. She took the bill slowly, as though she were afraid it was going to bite her or something, and carefully stuffed it inside the front of her blouse. How kin Ah evah tan k-yoo?"

"That's all right."

"Ah cud give you a blow job . . . "

"That's all right."

"It's wuth twenny dolla."

"That's all right."

THE END

94

Epilogue

"Maybe I was wrong about her age," I thought. "Maybe she really is sixteen."

THE FINAL END

Black and White

I've always been interested in sociology and anthropology and humanistic subjects like that. Also etymology, which is the study of word origins and their evolution, Maybe you could call etymology the anthropology of words. For instance, when I was taking a course in college on the History of Sub-Sahara Africa, I wondered about the origin of the words *Nigeria* and *Niger*. I figured that these words probably came from the word *negro,* because I had heard that many of the people who lived in those countries were Black, like African-Americans, or even blacker. I never found out the answer to that question for sure, but I did learn that, in the United States, *Nigger*, a word we are not supposed to use anymore, just means *Negro* in Black languages like Gullah or Geechee or other dialects. It wasn't always a bad word, not originally anyway. But I do know that the little country of Bantovia, which most Americans have never heard of, did get its name from the Bantu tribes so prevalent in that area of West Africa.

You see, in my senior year one of my classmates in a course of "Cultural Anthropology" was a very black exchange student from Bantovia. He explained the word origin to me, and a lot more. Mbumba Jareed was his name, and he was the blackest thing I had ever seen -- purple-ly black, like anthracite coal in the shade. He was proud of his pure black skin. Many of his countrymen, he told me, were not Black. Although most Americans did not know this, many Bantovians are said to be White. "I didn't

97

know many White people lived in Bantovia," I told him. "I thought that the people there who were not pure Black were dark people of mixed race, or Mulatto."

"Oh, we never use that word, *Mulatto*, like some of you do in the United States. Or used to anyway. And we don't have any Darkies, or Spades, or Coons, or Niggers, and only very few Jigaboos and Pickaninnies . In Bantovia we have only Blacks and Whites. If you are not Black you are White. Although the Whites are the minority, we try to give them full civil rights, including equal opportunity, every chance we get."

"Only Blacks and Whites?" I said as I sat there, incredulous and astonished, listening to Mbumba on the front steps of our main university library building. "You certainly must have a significant number of citizens of mixed blood, like Half-breeds, or Mestizos or something, even if you don't call them Mulattoes."

"Oh no we don't," insisted Mbumba. "In Bantovia, anybody who has a drop of white blood in his veins is White. Sometimes Whites who have some black blood try to pass for Black, but a careful observer can usually tell if he is really White, even though his skin may be almost as dark as mine. It may be partly a cultural thing, but even a drop of white blood can spoil the beautiful deep purplish tinge in the skin of a truly Black man. A couple of drops of white blood also makes their jaws weaker, their noses thinner, their hair straighter, and their arms and toes shorter. There are a lot of differences between Blacks and Whites besides skin, although in Bantovia it is illegal, or at least not politically correct, to mention these differences in the media or in public. You see, we try in every way we can to treat all Whites as our equals, even if some Whites don't appreciate it."

"I'd like to visit your country sometime."

"Why don't you come visit me this summer after we graduate? My job doesn't start until September, when the Legislature is back in session. I'll be working in my father's office in the Capitol; he's a senator and got me the job. I can show you around and we can pick some watermelons or go fishing for catfish on weekends."

So that's what I did. I spent six weeks with Mbumba, and wow, did I learn a lot! The first thing I learned was that Bantovia has almost no racial problems at all. And practically everybody I saw everywhere was Black, or so it seemed to me. "You're not being observant," said Mbumba. "Can't you see that their skin is not always black?" he insisted. Still, as far as I could tell, any of them who were not absolutely Black had skin as dark as unsweetened Hershey's chocolate, and that looked pretty black to me. Mbumba would also recite other racial differences. We took trips around the capital city and the countryside. We saw the Black House, where the president lives, with tall columns in front of the mansion, and a profuse tropical garden in back. We visited an orphanage filled with cute little "White" children who were born out of wedlock or whose poor parents could not afford to feed them, even though they all looked very black to me, as far as I could tell.

We visited the offices of the NAAWP, and I was impressed by the efforts of so many volunteers, mostly Blacks they were -- pure Blacks of course -- to help poor illiterate Whites with their education and career advancement. I learned about organizations and groups with names like White Panthers and White Power. One of the main avenues we strolled down was Martin Luther Boulevard. Mbumba explained that Martin Luther was a famous German priest who started a whole lot of Protestant sects and Evangelical churches, including two that evolved into today's Baptist Church and The Church of God in Christ, both of which are very vigorous in Bantovia.

I saw people in the Bazaar selling bumper stickers and banners reading, "White is Beautiful." I even learned about the kind of sperm-donors the Bantovian women choose if they are seeking artificial insemination. Reports showed that 85% of the women contacting the National Sperm Clinic preferred 100% black donors to father their children, even though at the same time some of these women were displaying "White Is Beautiful" signs on their front yards, automobiles, and schoolbooks. It sounded sort of hypocritical to me, but I guess we have hypocrites in the United States and other places as well.

At the capital, Mbumba Jareed's father, Senator Mkunga Jareed, was 100% pure purple black like Mbumba. In other words, he was even "Black" in Bantovia. He was a member of the White Caucus, a group of altruistic legislators devoted to the cause of full equal treatment for all the "White" citizens of Bantovia, especially those few who were 100% white, and accordingly needed the most help with their education and integration into society as productive members of the community. Hard as it is to believe, members of the White Caucus faced considerable opposition and animosity from other political colleagues who apparently did not see any advantage in it for themselves. The National White Urban League confronted similar problems and opposition from fringe racist groups that impeded their good works wherever possible. A few of these extremists went so far as to proclaim the Blacks a Master Race, even citing the words of Abraham Lincoln, who also adamantly opposed mixed marriages and declared that the races should be kept separated./1

But many Bantovians also view Lincoln's "Back to Africa" movement as an unfair disservice to the Bantovian nation and the pure Black Race, for with the re-diaspora, or deportation, of African Americans who had been slaves, or some of whose ancestors had been slaves, came many undesirable White genes into Bantovia. The vast majority of slaves in the United States in 1860 were not true Blacks, but were American Mulattoes who could not have passed

---

/1   In the Lincoln-Douglas Debates of 1858 Lincoln declared:

1) I am not, nor ever have been, in favor of qualifying Negroes and Whites to intermarry.

2)   There is a physical difference between the races, which I believe will forever forbid the two races living together.

3)   There must be the position of the superior and the inferior; and I, as much as any other man, am in favor of the superior position being assigned to ____ . (Here Lincoln mentioned one of the races.)

for Black in Bantovia where they would be seen as Whites. Bantovia has made great strides in overcoming these obstacles and difficulties, and the present Bantovian Government and society are foremost in the world in giving Whites rights and opportunities equal to those of the Blacks -- the true Blacks that is.

It is almost a color-blind society, except for a few do-good associations and activists who have to keep their eyes open to keep their jobs.

"I want to show you how far we have come," said Mbumba to me one day. "I want you to meet the President of Bantovia. He is a cousin of my mother's, but he is White. It was a long time before Bantovia was able to accept the idea of a White president, for that went against so much prejudice and racism that had burdened our history and lingered on through the years. The election of a White man to our presidency was a great leap forward for social justice and racial equality, even if he has not been able to do quite so much for our white citizens as they had hoped. He was cautious about creating political backlash if he showed overt favoritism to the Whites, so his policy was to continue to handle them as before. He vetoed an A.A. bill, you know, asserting that it was racist, if you can imagine that."/2

"Yes, I can understand why some people might feel that way," I said, hoping to sound interested and sympathetic but as non-committal as possible on the matter.

/2 Affirmative Action

So I met the President of Bantovia. He had even heard of me, to my delight. "Thank you for being a friend to Mbumba," he said. "He is like a son to me. I have always told him there is nobody you cannot learn something from, even a White boy."

"But you're . . . " I sort of stammered, not knowing what to say, as I remembered Mbumba's telling me the president had some white blood that made him White."

"Yes, I'm White too. Some of my mother's ancestors were slaves that Lincoln deported from the United States and sent to Bantovia and Liberia, so of course she had some white blood in her. Maybe it came from the *First Families of Virginia*, the *FFV*," he added with a chuckle.

I looked at Mbumba and back at the President. The difference in their skin color was hardly perceptible, if at all, like a pot and a kettle. And certainly his jaw didn't look any weaker or his nose any thinner than Mbumba's. Then Mbumba took me by the arm; it was time to go; the President was a busy man. "Thank you, Mr. President," we said, as I took his outstretched hand, as black as any I had ever seen anywhere, on the back side anyway. Amazing, I thought, that anyone could see any trace of White blood in him, let alone enough to call him White. Oh well, one drop is all it takes. He graciously thanked me for coming to visit his country as he bade us *adieu*.

Mbumba continued our conversation. "It was a great victory for the Liberals and the civil rights advocates to have a White president elected for Bantovia. With him in office we have had the best period the country has ever known. I wish you could stay on for a few more weeks; in September we celebrate White History Month."

THE END

Cheating

I knew I shouldn't do it -- really shouldn't be doing it. But what the heck, I will probably get away with it without anyone knowing. Or, as I should say, without *anyone's* knowing, to be grammatically correct.

Did you know that, with the use of gerunds in grammatical structures such as that one, the associated noun should be in the genitive case? Genitive means possessive. It is as though the *anyone* possesses the *knowing*, so it's anyone's knowing. That's what would be correct. But we are diverging from the story.

Another reason I decided I would go ahead and do what was on my mind, besides thinking that no one would ever know, is that in the past I had done some things. Of course, everything I have ever done was in the past. I haven't done anything in the future. Not yet. People talk about the present. Really, there is no such thing as the present. It doesn't exist. Everything is either past or future, sort of like prologue or epilogue. The present is instantaneous, with no duration in the time dimension. It is merely a point of inflection, as they say in calculus, an instant of change in direction or viewpoint. The crest of a hill. But that point is beside the point.

The point I was going to make is that I got away with doing some things in the past that I shouldn't have done. I let my school buddy Byron Matthews cheat from me on the algebra test and the Latin test, because he was bigger than I was and because he was my hero on the athletic field. He was a Big Man On Campus and I was just a little nerd that was a nobody, so it was an honor for me to have him recognize my presence and my existence and sit behind me and copy my answers on the algebra tests and the Latin tests. But we got away with it, I think. He ultimately atoned for our wayward behavior and our sinning by paying for it -- by paying rather heavily I thought -- he became an Episcopal priest. A new leaf.

Yes, he is an Episcopal priest, not an Episcopalian priest, as some people mistakenly say. *Episcopal* is the adjective, *Episcopalian* the noun. *Byron* is also a noun. A proper noun, that is. Very proper . . . now anyway.

THE END

The Toilet Seat Solution

Harry's Diner on Calumet Street was always busy at breakfast time. On weekdays, breakfast time started around 5:30 or 6:00 for day workers and construction crews, and even a few students or public school personnel getting an early start. But on Saturdays there was mostly a different type of clients, and the peak hours were between 8:30 and 10:30.

Harry's place wasn't elegant, or even fancy, but it had been there a long time, and Harry served a hearty breakfast at a reasonable price. He offered a standard menu with free grits on the side for any rare Southern ex-patriots who had wandered north to Sheboygan, Wisconsin looking for jobs at the city's famous Kohler porcelain and ceramics factory, and greasy hash-brown potatoes for anybody else.

Saturday mornings the clientele were different; they were mostly well-known old-timers, many retired, but some still working in positions of importance in business and local government and politics. There were always a few ribald jokes and banter, but these men also discussed serious demotic matters of interest concerning Sheboygan City and Sheboygan County. It was commonly believed around town that the men had a significant, albeit unofficial, role in "running Sheboygan." Even the mayor sometimes participated in this informal group, feeling his constituents' pulse, as it were. But nowadays *he* no longer came. <u>She</u> came.

107

Yes, the Democrats got in after the last election and installed a woman mayor, a new first. Margaret Battle already knew about this men's *kaffeeklatsch* and was socially acquainted with several of the men, and most of the wives. Many of the men in the group were, or had been, associated with the great Kohler Bath and Toilet factory, which dominated a suburb of Sheboygan, appropriately called Kohler. She knew that the company professed rigorous non-discrimination, for everything you can think of, to protect the downtrodden classes, including women and people with gender orientation. When she first swept into Harry's Diner at 9:15 one bright Saturday morning, the men could only gasp a little and try to catch their breath, but they couldn't do much about it.

Previously the tacit rule was that if you wanted to join the group you had to stand up for number one.

Recognizing that she was out-numbered and treading in new territory, Ms. Battle initially concentrated on trying to demurely hold her tongue and opinions to herself. For a while – for a few weeks – although it was difficult.

Then something happened.

The son of one of the Saturday morning regulars at Harry's surprised his father after school one day with the news that the Debating Society of North High School had chosen its subject for the Annual North High School Debate Challenge, namely, the interesting topic: "TOILET SEATS, UP OR DOWN?" The lad's name was Mark McKenzie; he was a senior at North and was in his third year on the debating team. Mark reported that the school

108

authorities overseeing the debating society planned to assigned roles, pro or con, "up" or "down," at random, to the participants, indiscriminately, boys or girls. They felt that would be democratic.

"But," said Mark to his father, "I don't think it's fair to make you take a side that you honestly do not agree with and honestly oppose."

So Mr. McKenzie had to explain to Mark that that was the idea behind true debating. A good debater should be able to argue any side of a question. "My own first wife could always do it; she loved to argue, and could argue anything, any direction, and often did just that," he asserted.

"Well," said Mark, "I think this question is too emotional. It would be better if it were simply the boys against the girls."

"No," said Mr. Mackenzie, "the argument is as old as Adam -- well, Adam and Eve anyway, or at least as old as the first toilet seats. And I doubt that it will ever be solved by taking sides or arguing. No, it will never be solved that way. But it's an interesting question. I think I'll ask the guys at Harry's on Saturday what they think."

"But Dad, like you said, we are not trying to answer the question, but just trying to test debating ability."

"Well, maybe it's not an appropriate subject. I'll ask them anyway." And so he did.

First thing next Saturday morning, McKenzie took the question to his buddies at Harry's. Ms. Battle had not yet arrived. "Good," thought McKenzie, who was known as Ken to his friends. "Listen guys," he started in, "there's something you ought to know about -- if you haven't heard already -- going on over at North High School." He then explained that his son had told him toilet seats were to be the subject of the debating contest.

"What's wrong with that?" said Mr. Allan Alderson, who had been Assistant Principal of North High School himself before he retired some ten years ago.

"Wrong with it? Toilet seats? Are you kidding? It's crazy," said Bill Bullock, "it will get in the news, and Sheboygan will get in the news, and we will be the laughing stock of the entire state, and maybe Minnesota and Illinois as well. The City Council should not allow it."

"The government is already poking its nose into places it has no business being, and not only gun control and health care," retorted Allan, who considered himself a somewhat-right-of-center conservative.

"But, Allan," piped up Vern Westergaard, his best friend, "you haf to dink of wat it might do to da morals und da social graces uff our yout, to haf dem talking about toilets like dis. It vudn't be at all nice, and certainly not consistent mit your own position on da importance uff upholdink American family values."

"Well, you know," said Corey Cunningham, who had been Vice President for Sales at the Kohler plant, "any

110

public discussion of toilet seats is bound to be good for Kohler. We are one of the biggest makers of toilets in the nation, and it would be a good thing to get more people immersed, or at least involved, in their toilets. It would be good business for the Kohler Company, and what is good for Kohler is good for Sheboygan and good for America."

"Sounds like I have heard that line before," said Deshay. "You are beginning to sound like Robert McNamara, when he was president of General Motors, before he took his theories and the rest of the United States into Vietnam."

"You're getting off the subject," said Eugene. "Let's go back to this toilet bowl debate at North High. What are we going to do about it?"

"Let's see what our sweet little mayor has to say. Is she coming today?"

"Don't ask me; I'm not her time-keeper. She's not my mayor anyway -- I never voted for her."

"She's still your mayor, whether you voted for her or not. I didn't vote for our president either, but he's still our president. Unfortunately."

"I was only speaking figuratively."

"I hope she does come," said Frank. "It may be best to get her on our side early on, if this thing is real. She is bound to be an important player in all this."

"On our side?" said Gregory Grabowski. "What do you mean? Have we taken sides already? I don't even know what the sides are."

"Look, as I see it," offered Hugh Harrup, "the question right now is whether filthy toilets are a proper subject for our children in high school to be sticking their heads into and to be talking about all the time."

"Hey, hold on there, Mister," said Mr. Irving Ingersol, a Kohler man. "Not all toilets are filthy, or even dirty. All our Kohler toilets are now made the E-Z-Kleen way, and for a little extra we also have a line of self-cleaning toilets with radiant omnicide for the seats themselves that you can buy for a slight additional charge -- for a fraction of what you cheapskates pay for whiskey every month."

"You never seemed to mind drinking my whiskey, Irving," said Phillip.

"Yeah, well you're special, Phil."

About that time Ms. Battle did arrive at Harry's. Harry himself hurriedly found her a comfortable seat in a central location, as a silent hush fell like a blanket over all the men. "Thank you Harry," said Ms. Battle, gently breaking the silence. But the silence returned and remained unbroken until, slightly peeved, she tried again, this time raising her voice until it was more like an Army sergeant's order than a request, "As you were, gentlemen!"

Mr. Ingersol, who had served briefly as Sheboygan City Clerk, jumped right in, apparently feeling it was his duty to smooth over any disruption caused by the mayor's incursion. "We want to welcome Ms. Battle this morning. She served our country as a United States Marine, you know. She has the right to go anyplace in Sheboygan she wants to, and she also has the right to be heard."

"Nobody said she didn't," responded two or three others. She's a person, isn't she?"

Mr. Ingersol turned toward Ms. Battle: We were only talking about toilet seats," he said, sounding somewhat embarrassed. "It's no big deal."

"Oh?" said Ms. Battle, "how interesting. I just love toilet seats myself," she said sarcastically, "especially when they are down," she added, hoping for a laugh, but getting only a mild forced chuckle.

Thereupon Ken and Mr. Irving Ingersol explained the problem as they saw it, that is, whether toilets are a suitable subject for debate at North High School. "Actually," began Ms. Battle, as do many people when they fear their views are not going to be well received -- "Actually, it sounds rather interesting, and if a debating contest is what it takes to make you men realize how important it is to we women, all over the world, for you men to leave the toilet seat in the 'down' position, where they were designed to be, then I am all in favor of the project. Besides, free speech is a good thing, and if it means that Kohler should make toilets with seats that automatically go back down, then so much the better."

113

"Madame," said Mr. Lansdown, one of the 'Kohler men', "thank you for your words. For your information, Kohler is already working on a prototype seat that will automatically return to its previous position after having been displaced for whatever purpose. Please come to our factory sometime, at your convenience, and let us give you a demonstration -- or even a trial if you prefer."

"Sounds as though that might be rather fun," she said with a laugh, hoping by her humor to gain a few supporters for the views she would be offering.

* * * * *

These conversations continued for a few more Saturdays, with the general consensus being that there wasn't much anybody could do about the Debate Contest plans, even if they wanted to. Some, like the mayor, were interested in the substance, and thought they would like to see how the controversial issue might turn out in a full debate.

Meanwhile, back at North High School, the contest designers focused on a matter of more immediate concern, namely whether it was "fair" to assign contestants to sides, pro or con, "up" or "down" at random. Left-leaning Democrats, like the mayor, felt that random assignments would be a fair and traditional way for organizing debates. However, most Republicans and other right-wingers saw that as violating the idea of freedom of speech and some Amendment or other.

Accordingly, the organizers took a poll of the "North High School Family," which comprised students and their parents and siblings, present and past faculty and administrative personnel at the school, alumni and alumnae, past donors to the school Development Fund, and a few other categories as well. Most residents of Sheboygan therefore were connected in some way to North High School. Poll participants were allowed to remain anonymous, giving only age and gender orientation. The results overwhelmingly favored choice, even among people from Republican families that had never before voted for anything with "choice" in it in their life. The poll showed overwhelming support for "choice," regardless of the gender or orientation of the respondent.

When the debates were getting started and the choices were actually made, by contestants as to which side, "up" or "down," they would debate on, it turned out, as expected, to be boys against girls, or "men versus women," as they preferred to say, with only a few crossing normal gender lines -- perhaps a few extreme liberals and a few from the LGBT community who also had felt that random assignment would have been fair. These folk were ready to debate either side of the question, as true debaters should be. Some of them did not even indicate their own gender or gender preference in their questionnaire. One simply gave "American" for his/her/its gender. Two or three of them wrote in "other," and there was one who said "alien." So maybe, after all, they would get a bit of a mix, even while letting contestants choose sides. So that's what they did; contestants would be allowed to chose their side.

When it came time for the debates, the girls of course all argued in favor of "down" and the boys almost unanimously in favor of "up" – all but three who voted with their sisters out of chivalrous respect for the ladies, or because their mothers had ordered them to do so. "After all," said one of the mothers, "this is supposed to be a test of how good a debater you are, and taking the 'down' side will be a realistic challenge for you."

The "down" arguments focused largely on the discomfort to a woman if she had to go in a hurry, for instance on a dark and stormy night, when she was sleepy and couldn't find the light switch. Also there was support for the contention that chivalry required some masculine attention to woman's comfort in times of need or stress. Others pointed out the possibility of women breaking their fingernails if they always had to put the seat down by themselves. Or that, if the seat slipped and banged freely down from its insecure "up" position, the noise might wake the baby. Some even offered the penetrating argument that the toilet looked nicer if the seat were down whenever there were elegant guests invited for dinner, possibly including elegant ladies who might want to use the facility.

There was also the contention that it would be fair if boys, and men too, were taught to sit whenever they went to the john, for whatever purpose -- yes, that would be fair. Just like the old days, when the best of homes had out-houses for this sort of thing, which, whether one-holers or two-holers, generally had no soft plastic seats or lids at all, so everything was fair and square, even if the holes themselves were approximately round.

One very neutral argument that was touched upon -- I am not sure which side brought it up -- suggested that modern homes should have "His" and "Hers" toilets, adjacent in a

116

friendly fashion like the useless redundant double washbasins many present-day mass-produced American homes now have to make them look high class. Another suggested two bathrooms in every home, for "Gents" and "Ladies" respectively and respectfully, with appropriate doggie heads painted on the doors, representing "Pointers" and "Setters," also respectively. But the best contention was that it would be fair if men were taught to sit whenever they went to the john, for whatever purpose. Yes, that would be fair. It is easier for men to sit down than for women to stand up.

There were just as many arguments favoring the "up" position, such as the observation that if a man had to micturate, or do number one/1 in a hurry on a dark night, he might not have time to raise the seat, and accordingly he might unintentionally leave a little inadvertent collateral spray slightly besmirching the seat in his haste. "Well, if he does that, he should wipe the seat clean," someone would say. "But do you really think you can always count on him to do that?" Men are not very good at wiping up, even after themselves, in spite of any sympathetic thoughts or concern they could have had for the damsel who may be following them. And if he used Clorox it would make the seat slippery, and the aroma would conflict with the ladies'

/1 In our house, when we were kids, we liked to say "micturating" and "defecating," because that's exactly what you were doing, and we liked using big words we had learned in school. But Mom didn't like that. She said they were ugly and sounded "uncouth," and ever since then she made us say number one and number two because it sounded more elegant. You know, more refined. More high class.

perfume. It was indeed with the benefit and comfort of the damsel in mind, that men usually put the seat "up" in the first place.

The debates thereupon took place just about as the organizers had conceived them, with one important difference. The contest and the controversy it arose appeared less and less to be a test of one's oratory ability and logic and debating style, but more of a quest to determine what, or who, was right: "Up" or "Down."

At least that's the way the media liked to see it, and much of the public as well, as the debate spilled out from the North High School auditorium, all over town and across the county, into book groups and coffee shops, library discussion groups, and even some old folks' homes, now called retirement communities or assisted living -- if the inmates were not too old to follow the ups and downs of it all. So, the results of the contest were inconclusive.

But that's not all. The *Milwaukee Journal Sentinel* had gotten interested in these "Sheboygan Shenanigans," as they called them, and offered a $5,000 prize for the person, either man or woman, or unspecified, who was not necessarily the best orator, but who offered the best solution (to the problem). They were interested in WHAT, not HOW. Many letters and articles had already been in the local press and a few had begun to appear in the national press as well (even the *Washington Post* on a slow day). Most media outside of Sheboygan and southeastern Wisconsin took the matter as a big joke, including some of the late-hour TV comedians, but in Sheboygan and Kohler it was no joking matter -- it was serous business.

118

Finally a chap from South High School, to the chagrin of the organizers, who were all associated with North High School -- hit upon the answer; he mailed his solution to the editor of the *Milwaukee Journal Sentinel*, and won the $5,000, plus an interview on WCSC TV.

His name, appropriately enough, was Solomon. Solomon Gerber. Solomon had been in England for his Junior Year Abroad, and was now a senior at South. In England toilets are known as Water Closets, or WC's. Solomon knew what a closet was, and what WC meant, but out of curiosity he looked up "closet" in the Oxford English Dictionary. Therein he read that the word "closet" is, *inter alia*, a verb that means "to shut." Now, thinking back on his experience in England, and considering the present real situation, Solomon suddenly put 2 and 1 together, and announced loudly to himself, "*Eureka!*" which means "I have found it" in Greek, at least in the Greek of Aristotle's day. So he sent in his solution to the newspaper and won the $5,000 prize.

When he got on TV, he explained that, because his name was Solomon, his first idea was to suggest that toilet seats should be cut in half, longitudinally, with one half being the property of the men, to do what they wanted to with it, and one half being the property of the women to use as they saw fit. He went on to say that nobody liked this idea except perhaps the half-assed people who organized the stupid debate in the first place.

So then he explained his winning idea: "If a WC is a water closet, and a closet is something that can be shut, then the solution is simply to require people of whatever

119

gender orientation to shut the toilet lid after use, as was perhaps originally intended. The next person, of whatever gender, will open the lid, with or without lifting the seat, depending on his, or her, or its, taste and preference, and accordingly close the lid upon termination of functions. So, as the Looney Tunes character used to say, 'That's all, folks!' QED."

(Roars of applause from the TV studio audience.) Then the TV studio MC, before closing, broke in and said, "Thank you, Solomon. You are well named. Congratulations."

THE END

Pacific Triangle

Throughout the 19th century, as well as before and after that brief hundred years, the islands of the South Pacific were fascinating, exotic, even mysterious distant lands in the eyes of Europeans and other advanced societies. Magellan and Cook thought they were delightful gems in another world. Portuguese and Dutch explorers, Vasco Da Gama, Abel Tasman, and others, saw not only beauty but, early on, began to realize the commercial potential and, yes, the religious potential, of many of these islands. Commercial opportunities lay in the trade of material goods, trinkets and whisky, in exchange for native art works, spices, exotic fruit and vegetables, and even precious metals. Religious opportunities lay in the possibilities for bringing in Christianity to save the untutored souls of the heathen natives.

Caleb Morgan was born in Europe in the Old Country. He was the son of an energetic Protestant minister and grew up in a devout religious atmosphere. At the appropriate time in the course of his education, Caleb entered a religious seminary and in due course became an ordained minister himself, following in his father's footsteps. But unlike his father, who had devoted his energies to caring for the souls of his neighbors and fellow countrymen, Caleb felt there were other souls in greater need of salvation in distant lands where Christianity was unknown. Caleb decided to become a missionary and devote *his* energies to tending to the souls of heathen men who had never heard

121

of the saving power of the grace of our Lord Jesus Christ, and the souls of heathen women who had never even learned to cover their bare breasts. After considerable study and reflection on the matter, or maybe because God spoke to him in a dream, Caleb concluded that the Tuamoto Islanders in the South Pacific were the people to whom he was destined to bring salvation.

Caleb moved to Vanu Mentrist Atoll, in the Tuamoto Islands, bag and baggage, and set up shop. He had a lot of work to do to make these fun-loving, happy-go-lucky people take life seriously, and change their sinful ways that had been leading them to Hell and Damnation. It wasn't only women going about with their tits hanging out. Men and women lived on and off together in a big ensemble, and came and went with aplomb, so to speak. All the adults cared for all the children of the village, for you never knew which ones might be your own, at least if you were a man. Caleb instituted the beauty of the marriage rite, explaining the joy of faithfully living to death with one and the same spouse. Divorce was not in his vocabulary.

To demonstrate a proper lifestyle and marriage, Caleb took for himself, as his bride, the teen-age daughter of the Village Chief. In due course she bore two daughters that Caleb was pretty sure were his own. Gloria and Rosilyn their names were, and, like their father, they received as rigorous a religious upbringing as he was able to give them. They were not allowed to pierce their noses with dolphin bones, or wear grass skirts with nothing under them, or to use transparent material for their bathing suit tops after he had forbidden topless attire. They learned to bless the food at every meal, go to church three times a week and twice on

Sunday, and never to hold hands or anything with boys, or ever to look at boys when they took off their clothes to go swimming.

But the Devil got into the girls nevertheless, as He so often does, and they could not resist looking at a well developed naked male even when they knew they were not supposed to. Women had always been like that, for generations. The girls were quite sure that they liked looking at boys naked, but when they learned about Hell, they were not sure they wanted to go on looking so much. It might not be worth the risk; that is, if looking at naked boys might mean you could go to Hell. Nevertheless, in spite of those odds, they often risked it, and took a peek when the opportunities presented themselves, just as their mothers had done when *they* were young girls. And the image was etched in their mind's eye in spite of their efforts -- admittedly modest efforts -- to dispel it.

Caleb would have liked to have a son or two whom he might have made into missionaries in his own image. But no luck; he had to make do with the two daughters, Gloria and Rosilyn. He would have liked for them at least to become nuns one day, and carry on the work of stamping out irreverent vulgarity. He gave them the best religious education he could, home schooled of course. They served as his choir, his altar-boys, his vicars and curates and sextons -- whatever sextons are. They visited the sick with him, prayed for the dead and dying with him, and helped him bury the dead, after they had died.

He also taught them to care for each other, and made them swear never to touch a man or a boy improperly, and never to look at them between the waist and the knees. They were dutiful daughters, and, in spite of their mother's tacit concerns that they were missing some of the joys of life, they followed their father's path and teachings to a tee.

The girls never became nuns, but they did live a restricted and holy religious life. When their parents died, the girls, who were now 28 and 31 years old, went on living together and taking care of each other in holiness and righteousness.

The villagers all knew the Morgan sisters were weird; that is to say, everyone knew they were holy virgins. The village women admired and respected their purity, but did not envy it. The dirty old men of the village, as well as some relatively young ones, knew it was a waste of time ever to try to make out with one of the Morgan sisters. They were indeed good girls. By then, no one ever bothered them anymore. With their father's vision still etched upon their inward eye, the sisters decided to honor their father's memory and ensure their own salvation. Accordingly, they removed themselves from the life of sinful temptations that had been surrounding them, and, completely deracinated, retreated to a tiny, uninhabited, atoll nearby, hardly more than a sandbar with a couple of palm trees. They planned to spend the rest of their lives together there, giving themselves over entirely to God and to His Blessed Son, in isolated contemplation and prayer, in holiness and righteousness, for the rest of their days, ensuring their everlasting purity and eternal salvation.

*   *   *   *   *

Milton Durant was three or four years younger than the Morgan sisters, but didn't know them -- not at first, and not for a long time, for he was born and raised in Charleston, South Carolina, a good distance from Vanu Mentrist Island in the Tuamotos. Charleston, as you know, is an important seaport, and also a major yachting center, on the Atlantic coast. Young Milton, or Milt as his friends knew him as, loved the ocean, the beach, and the salt air, but especially he loved boats of all kinds. You see, Milt was the son of a boat builder, and growing up, he spent many hours messing about in the boatyard, talking to the workmen, playing with their children, and of course learning to sail. The boatyard was next to the yacht club, where Milton regularly competed in weekend sailing races as well as in major regattas and ocean races against competitors from all over the southeastern part of the United States.

So he was healthy and vigorous, and he knew boats, and was a good sailor, winning many trophies and awards. He was blond and fair, so he used plenty of suntan cream and long-sleeved shirts. By the time he was in his early twenties and had finished college, he had done almost everything a young Charleston yachtsman could do. Almost. There was one more thing he needed to do before he settled down and got a job and got married and started raising a family, like a proper Southern gentleman. He needed to sail around the world. Milton recalled one of his friends' having once called him a sissy because he would not stand up and fight a school bully who had picked on him and knocked him down because he didn't like his hat. Milton wasn't really a sissy; he just didn't like fighting. "I'll show them who's a sissy," he thought, as he began to make his plans for the circumnavigation.

Milton Durant had read Joshua Slocum's book, *Sailing Alone around the World*, and many other books by ocean sailing adventurers. His heroes were the ones who had circumnavigated the world since the days of Ferdinand Magellan. Many of us forget that Magellan did not make it; he was killed in the Philippines by angry natives. Of his original fleet of five vessels, only one survived the arduous undertaking and returned to Europe under the command of Sebastian Elcano, a young Spaniard who is still a famous hero in the Basque country. Milton also read about the adventures of Sir Francis Chichester, Robin Knox Johnston, Chay Blythe, and Bernard Moitessier, each of whom had managed to circumnavigate the globe single handed.

Milton's father was all for it. He would provide the boat and finance the trip. The advertising value for his boatyard would be worth it. Mrs. Durant was not so keen on the idea; she "could not picture her baby" out there on the ocean all by himself, but she was only a feather in a high wind and easily overruled. But she did make some sandwiches for him to take along.

After many weeks of preparation -- months actually -- Milton finally got it all together and set off for Panama one fine day in November after hurricane season was over. Milton was not trying to set a lot of new records, like single-handed distance records. He would stop along the way for rest, relaxation, provisions, and curiosity about the local people. He stopped in Nassau, which he knew from several ocean races. He stopped in San Juan; he stopped in Curaçao to see the beach and try the rum and cokes. By the time he got to Panama and went through the canal, he was feeling comfortable in his solitary life at sea, and felt ready for a long passage with no land in sight, all the way to the Tuamoto Islands.

Now the most difficult thing about the Tuamoto Islands is that they are badly marked on the charts and are hard to see, with no elevation more than fifty feet above sea level. Approaching vessels can be on top of them almost before they can see them. Milton wisely planned his first landfall for midday, when the islands would be most clearly visible.

But then something happened.

Whether the east wind at Milton's back was stronger than he realized, or whether there was an extreme eastern outlier island not on the charts of the Tuamotos, Milton never knew. The night before his intended landfall, or rather, early in the morning before sun-up, he was hit by a violent, unanticipated northeasterly storm, rare that time of year in those latitudes. Milt brought down his mainsail, leaving up only the tiny storm jib, and hove to, to ride it out. But he didn't make it. Shortly before dawn his boat crashed upon the volcanic reef surrounding a tiny atoll that Milton did not know existed. The vessel was smashed to pieces and sank quickly. Milt was hit in the head when the mast fell, kocking him unconscious.

Fortunately he had taken the precaution of donning his life-vest when the storm first threatened the night before. He was washed overboard, or perhaps the vessel just sank from under him. He was unconscious, but his life-vest held him face-up in the water. Three hours later, when the morning sun was well above the horizon, the water washed his body ashore on a sandy beach, with him still in it.

127

* * * * *

"Oh my, what is that!" were the first words that came to the ears of Milton Durant.

"Where?"

"Over there. It looks like . . . Oh Dear . . . I think it's a human body."

"It looks like Goldilocks," said Gloria.

"No, it's got no tits. It's . . . Oh my, it's a man. I can tell. See?"

"Maybe he's still alive; he wasn't here yesterday."

With that, the two compassionate young women dragged him to the shade of a nearby palm-tree. By then, Milton was beginning to come to and beginning to wonder what was going on. "What's going on?" he muttered through his parched lips.

"Run get him some water; he may be thirsty. I'll stay here and see that he doesn't get away."

Rosilyn came back with some coconut juice that she thought this strange visitor might like better than plain water. She found Gloria sitting cross-legged with the blond head resting cosily in her lap. She was brushing the flies away from a little bloody spot on his forehead and looking tenderly into his eyes as his eyelids were just beginning to flutter.

128

"He's alive, Rosie. He's alive! I think he was sent to us from Heaven. God wants us to take care of him."

"What's going on? Where am I?" muttered the beautiful blond stranger, speaking English.

"You are here," said Gloria, also speaking English, slowly and clearly, as her father had taught her to do.

"You are with us," said Rosilyn, further elaborating on her sister's comment. "Here, drink this."

The two young women could see that the man was not used to being washed up on topical beaches, and that he seemed confused, as though he wasn't sure where he was. They tacitly agreed not to ask him too many questions right away, but devoted themselves to tending to his physical condition. They were excited to note that he was a well developed young man for his size, but obviously had been through a stressful experience recently. They supported him under his arms and took him back to their little house -- just a straw shanty, really.

There they cared for his wound with demulcent banana paste, washed his body clear of the salt and sand, fed him some soup and coconut bread soaked in coconut milk, and laid him out to rest on the most comfortable palm-leaf mat they had. Then with some reluctance and mixed emotions they covered his midriff and loins with a cloth made from palm fibers, knowing that that's what their father would have wanted them to do. Then they brushed away the flies so he could sleep longer, until he regained his strength.

129

"I think the one true God has given us a gem," said Gloria. "He looks like God Himself, in His one true image, don't you think?"

"Oh yes," said Rosilyn, "and God has given us the responsibility of caring for him."

"I think he's cute. I wouldn't mind caring for him myself."

"Me neither. Do you think we could both care for him?"

"Well, we are both caring for him now, aren't we?"

"I meant. You know . . . take *care* of him. Father said that when a man and a woman grow up and want to be together there are special things that they can do, but it has to be just one man and just one woman."

"Well, there is just one man here."

"We are going to have to think about this. Maybe there is some way we can work it out. But for now . . . Look, he's waking up."

"Let's find out who he is and what part of Heaven he came from."

Milton knew something had happened. He was sure of it, although he didn't quite know exactly what. He realized he had been asleep. Now, still only half awake, he reached to his sore forehead and got sticky banana paste on his fingers. "No, don't touch it," said a sweet Polynesian voice with a British accent, as a cool hand held his wrist. "You must let it get well." Gloria had meant to say, "Let it heal," but couldn't remember the word "heal." Her English wasn't perfect, but what she did know was quite good; Reverend Caleb had seen to that. "You have had a bump on the head, but don't worry, I am going to take care of you."

"WE are going to take care of you," said her sister, Rosilyn, insisting on getting in on the act and touching his shoulder while gently stroking his forearm. "My name is Rosilyn," said Rosilyn. "That's my sister Gloria. What's your name?"

The man seemed to hesitate. "Could I have another glass of water?" he said, "I seem to be thirsty . . . my name? Is that what you asked me?"

"Yes," said Rosilyn gently. "What's your name?"

"My name . . . " he said slowly, "my name is Milt . . . Yes, that's it, Milt. Milton Durant. I'm sure that's it."

"Where are you coming from?" asked Gloria this time.

"Coming from?" Milton Durant seemed confused.

"Yes, where are you coming from? Where is your home?"

"I . . . I'm not sure. Let me think a minute." Well, one minute ran to two, to five, to sixty. "I know what you are asking, and I'm sure I know. I mean I do know where I'm

131

from -- I have it on the tip of my tongue, but just can't remember right now."

Well, all that day, and even the next day, he still couldn't remember. Apparently, Milton Durant had some kind of amnesia from the blow to his head. He was lucky to be alive; lucky these sweet young maidens had found him and had so kindly soothed him and re-hydrated his desiccated body.

"I know where he's from," said Gloria, moving even closer to Milton. "He's from Heaven, aren't you Milt? God sent you here to be with me."

"To be with *us*," injected Rosilyn. "I'm here too, you know. Maybe I'm the one He sent him here to be with." Milt was feeling much better now, with all this pulchritudinous attention, and, in spite of his weakened state, was beginning to get somewhat aroused. That was when Rosilyn noticed that the palm coverlet they had placed over his chest and thighs seemed to be undergoing a slight movement or displacement from some force below. Without any deep thinking about what she was saying, Rosilyn popped out with, "He's a pretty big boy; maybe he is big enough for both of us."

"Oh, how can you say such a thing? You know that Father said one man must be for only one woman that way."

"Oh, I didn't mean all that. I just meant around the house," she lied.

"You and I will have to have a quiet talk," said Gloria in a hushed voice, not wanting Milt to know they were talking about him. Then they turned their attention back to Milton's face.

"Do you remember anything else?" said Rosilyn. "I mean your family, where you were born, or where you learned English? Our Father, I mean our Dad -- *that* father -- came here from far away to teach us English."

"To HAVE us, AND to teach us English," corrected Gloria.

Milt stirred some more. "I remember water. There was water all around me, and under me, and I was thirsty but I couldn't drink it. It was all salt water. That's about all I remember right now."

Over the next few weeks Milton began to remember a few more things. He had been on a boat -- a sailboat. He was taking a long trip but could not remember either his departure point or his destination. He had serious amnesia, but didn't seem too upset about it. His forehead sore had cured, and he had no more headache. He was getting accustomed to the simple life on this little island, healthful food, mostly comprising tropical fruit and fish; and two lovely women to give him back-rubs and massages, and play with him, and teach him about the island. When his strength and vigor returned, he even imagined it might be more fun if there were only one such maiden, without an ever-present chaperon, but it would not be fair for him to play favorites, so he did nothing. That is to say, he restrained his inchoate innate urges to propound any romantic overtures. Furthermore, the two women, usually together and ever-watchful of each other, made sure he had no such opportunities to pursue mono-zygote-gametic advances with one of them in any case.

"We have to have a talk," Gloria would say to Rosilyn from time to time, as she was ever more frequently touched by her thoughts and imaginings to have Milt to herself for a lifetime. Or even for a little while, like all to herself right now for an hour or two. She liked her sister Rosilyn, she really did. Loved her even. For many months she was the only other person she had known, or even seen. But a man -- that would be something different, she thought, as the normal physical urges of this healthy young woman continued to stir about and bubble up closer and closer to the surface. She was sorry her father had so instilled in her the knowledge that it would be a gross sin -- he might have called it a "mortal sin" or a "deadly sin" -- for any really hot romantic activity to take place between a man and woman who were not committed and bound to this single and sole relationship, "forsaking all others," as he put it.

"Well," thought Gloria, "I can forsake all others -- even all other men -- with no problem. I couldn't do otherwise if I wanted. No men here. But what about Milt? Would he always ignore Rosilyn's attractions?" (She did not know about the way some other people, like Mormons, for instance, might resolve such a problem.) "But these are all moot points, because Rosilyn would never let me have Milt all to myself. She would at least want a piece of him, or all of him, if she could. Well, so would I. We have to have a talk."

So the first thing she said when she woke up the next morning was, "Rosie, we have to have a talk."

"All right, about what?"

"Ya know, Milton's a man."

"Yes, I've noticed."

"He's a man, and you and I are women."

"I'm aware of that too."

"He's a man and he's going to waste. And you and I aren't getting any younger either."

"All right. What are you driving at?"

"Something has to happen. There are powerful forces between men and women, you know, after they become adults and start maturing."

"I think I know what you mean. You mean, like, romantic forces, lascivious inclinations, and inner urges."

"Yes, exactly. You took the words right out of my mouth. I've had the same feelings, and it's getting harder and harder for me to suppress them, especially as I get older, and think about Milt, and look at him, and think about him some more. What do you think we should do?"

"I don't know. What's your idea?"

135

"I can imagine four possibilities: First, we could go on living a life free from sin and ignore this outstanding opportunity offered by Milt and Heaven to savor the joy of the Real Thing. Second, we could share him, taking turns doing the business whenever Milton wanted one of us, like the Egyptian Sultans did with the women in their harems in the olden days."

"Oh my, but they were infidels. That might lead us onto the Path to Hell. You mean you would really do that?"

"Maybe. It would certainly be tempting. Anyway, nobody would have to know.."

"God would know."

"How do you know that?"

"He knows everything. Father said so. All right, so what are Three and Four?"

"Three is you get him all for yourself, and Four is I get him. Four is best, because I am older than you and I will probably die before you do, and then you can have the rest of him all for yourself."

"He might be all used up and finished off by then."

"No. The books say men can go on and even become fathers of new babies at a much more advanced age than women can," said Gloria, showing off her knowledge and choosing her words carefully.

136

"I wasn't really thinking about babies. Anyway, I'm not just going to let you have him like that. I have as much right to him as you do. Besides, I saw him first."

"No, I saw him first."

"I have an idea."

"What?"

"It has to be Three or Four. Let's flip for it."

"You mean, like, toss a coin?"

"Yes, sure."

"We can't do that."

"Why not?"

"It would be gambling, and that's against the Bible -- I think. Bedsides, I haven't got a coin. Have you?"

"Well, no . . . So much for that idea . . .

"Tell you what."

"What?"

"I'll hold a flat pebble in one hand and a round one in the other, and you choose, and if you guess the right one, you win, and if not, I win."

So that's what they did. The winner could have Milt come visit her in her hut whenever she wanted him to, and the loser would stay away and not bother them. Milton wasn't consulted. He never regained all his marbles after getting hit in the head by the broken mast, and now he would do almost anything Gloria or Rosilyn told him to do. If they said lie down he would lie down; if they said stand up he would stand up. They were sure that if they told him to do *something* he would do *something*. He was a good man. He even smiled when they told him to smile.

That arrangement went on for many years, with the loser always keeping her distance and staying in her own hut whenever she thought her sister and Milt might want to be together, like, intimately. Milt also had his own hut, so he could be alone when he wanted to. He spent many hours trying to remember where he came from and who his family had been. But he was not unhappy on this tropical island with lots of sunshine and the added pleasures of delicious tropical fruit and fresh fish.

Then when he was barely entering middle age, he suddenly died. He hadn't meant to. Apparently, as a result of the blow to his head years before, a brain tumor had begun to grow, which went on and subsequently took his life in such an untimely fashion.

Gloria and Rosilyn were quite grief stricken and also heartbroken. It was indeed "disheartening and demoralizing"/1 to see this wonderful God-given creature

---

/1 to use the words of Judge Gorsuch, February, 2017

lying there dead before their eyes -- this man who had brought so much richness into the lives of both of them, but especially into the life of one of them, the lucky one who had won the pebble toss so many years ago, the toss that gave her exclusive nighttime love of the man and his body for half a lifetime.

"Oh dear," said Gloria with tears in her eyes, "I'm going to miss him."

"Oh dear," said Rosilyn with her throat chocked up with sorrow, "I am going to miss him. And I'm so sorry for you too, my Dear, for I know you are going to miss him."

"Yes, that's what I said. But I can only imagine how hard it will be for you."

Then one of them said, "If you had died instead of him, I would have loved him and taken care of him for the rest of his life, you know."

"Of course you would have. And I know he appreciated all you did for him when he was alive."

"I envied you, you know."

"You envied me? Because I always kept my virginity?"

"YOUR virginity? Are you out of your mind? Do you have amnesia too? I was the one who kept MY virginity, although I never chose to do so."

And so the discussion continued, for as the reader has by now surmised, there was misunderstanding with the famous toss of the coin, or rather the choice of the flat or round pebble.

"But you drew the flat one . . . You won!"

"But you drew the round one! YOU won, I lost."

"Oh dear, I thought I lost."

"Dear me, I thought I lost."

Do you mean . . . ?" "Do you mean . . . ?" they said almost in unison.

Yes, that's what they meant. They had both faithfully foregone the opportunity of a lifetime to lie down alongside a man, each thinking she had lost the draw and that it was the other who, all these years, had been continually enjoying life-after-virginity. "I thought that you , , ," "I thought that you . . ."

"Dear Lord," they said, "we have failed to properly receive and enjoy the gift that You in Your bounty sent into our lives, and we want to say that we are sorry. Very sorry. Amen."

"Yes, we are very sorry. Very very sorry. Amen."

"Amen. Ah , , , men!"

THE END

Divide and Conquer

Mediators and counselors may do more than just try to keep a married couple together. If divorce is inevitable, a mediator may help ease the process, save money from lawyer fees and court costs, and help arrive at a division of common assets satisfactory to both parties, or as near thereto as possible.

Herbert and Priscilla Geldlieben wisely chose to work with a mediator when they were splitting up.

Herbert, with his nice Ipana smile and his good taste in Italian neckties, made quite a bit of money in real estate, while Priscilla ran the household and helped to entertain Herbert's clients, as well as take care of his Alzeimers-ridden mother until she died last year. The couple owned a nice house in the suburbs and had investments worth $3,400,000.

Priscilla didn't want the house with its unpleasant memories, but she did want a big share of the money, and that is where they couldn't agree. She felt that she had, in her way, contributed just as much as he had to the marriage, even more, and she wanted money. He could have the house.

After days of arguing they went to a mediator and continued to argue for a few more days. The mediator suggested that her share should be $1,700,000. Neither of them liked that. The mediator, who had a law degree and was a notary public as well, said, "You have to agree on something." But the arguing went on.

Finally, in apparent exasperation, Priscilla said, "All right, just divide my share by 1/2 and give me the money, and I will fly to Mexico next week and be out of your hair, and out of your life forever."/1

That sounded petty good to Herbert, so he immediately turned to the mediator and said, "That's fine. Write it up just as she said."

The mediator raised her eyebrows and asked, "You mean that? Are you sure?"

"Yes, yes, just as she said. I want this over with; I am sick and tired of the whole thing," asserted Herbert.

*　*　*　*　*

On the plane to Mexico, Priscilla did some calculating./1 "Let's see," she said, "$400,000 will be enough for a nice house, and the rest invested at three per cent should give me about $90,000 a year income. I can live on that."

THE END

/1 To the reader: What does 1,700,000 divided by 1/2 equal? Are you sure?

Second Street, a Painting

Lewis Gallagher was my second husband, and my best one. I'm Courtney. Lewis and I were very happy together, for quite a number of years.

Then something frightful happened.

When we got back home after a week "mini vacation" at Lake George over in New York State, the worst of all possible nightmares came true. Our home had been broken into. Burglarized. We had been robbed.

"Oh my God!" I think I screamed, coming in the front door. "Somebody has broken in here! We've been burglarized! Oh Dear!"

Lewis came in right behind me, and his immediate reaction was quite similar to my own. "Holy Cow," he said firmly and quite clearly, apparently agreeing with me wholeheartedly. "It looks like we've been robbed. I wonder what they were looking for. Do you see anything missing?" he said, just as horrified and dumbfounded as I was, maybe more so.

"Look," I said, "the carpet's gone. My beautiful, red Boukara carpet with the elephant-foot pattern that was my grandmother's. See?" I added for emphasis; "Look, it's gone! It was right there," I said, shocked and tearful, pointing to a bare area in the middle of the living room floor.

143

Thereupon we rapidly rushed around the house to see what else was missing, or rather, to see what we couldn't see because it wasn't there. Stolen. "We'd better call the police," I wisely suggested. So Lewis called 911.

"Was anybody hurt?" they wanted to know.

"No. We were away. Nobody was here," Lewis said.

"When did it happen? Do you know who did it?"

"No, I'm telling you, no one was here."

"You'd better report it to the police."

"I thought that that was what I was doing. Then, can you switch me to the police? Or give me their number or something?" Lewis was speaking more loudly than necessary, for, like me, he was completely devastated by this devastating turn of events, and quite irritated.

So the police asked some of the same questions, and then helpfully added, "Yes, there have been quite a few burglaries around the County lately. You have to be careful." They finally ended by telling us to submit an itemized list of stolen items, preferably with photographs, and with identifying marks and estimated value, as soon as possible, and "we'll see what we can do."

Ever more distraught, the two of us spent the evening going through the house looking for things that weren't there. "The TV's gone, but the CD's and VCR's are still here." "Yeah, who wants CD's and VCR's anymore anyway?" (The only reason Lewis kept the old TV was to play his old VCR's and his old CD's.)

Our new multi-functional microwave oven was gone, and the imported automatic Italian espresso coffee maker was also gone, as were our pair of sterling silver candelabra and the tea service set (which was only silver plate, however). And Lewis's 0.22 Mossberg target rifle that he used to shoot tin cans with, but never shot in anger, was gone too. But he was angry now, and so was I, and we were upset too. They had taken various other items, but had kindly left the fridge, the stove, and our pickup truck.

And then Lewis screamed. Quite loudly. Penetratingly. I thought for a minute that he must have twisted his old broken ankle, going up the step to his study. "It's gone," he wailed. "Second Street is gone! They have stolen Second Street!" ("Second Street" was the name of a painting of a street in Stockbridge, Massachusetts.)

It is a terrible thing, a terrible feeling, to have your house broken into. Devastating. If you are a woman it is the feeling I imagine you might have if you were violated. It's like a nightmare where someone catches you out naked, someone you don't even know. Helpless. Unfair. Evil. Horrible.

*   *   *   *   *

As I started to say, Lewis was my second husband. My first was a big mistake that I don't even want to go into now. That's another story. But Lewis was, and is, my True Love, my salvation, and I loved him all the more for what I had suffered before he came into my life. He too had been married before, to a distant cousin of mine, Inge Danforth, who I didn't know very well, and I didn't much like even what I did know of her way back then.

After my own divorce I had been back living for a time with my parents in their house outside of New Haven. I had a job there, with my father's company, a resurrected paper mill, that was doing pretty well, but I was getting older, almost 30, and still unmarried. Or rather, *again* unmarried.

It was my mother who brought Lewis into my life. When she was in her 'teens and a student at Rosemary Hall she had a friend at Choate named Paul Gallagher. My mother apparently liked the whole Gallagher family quite a lot; over the years they kept in touch and she watched Paul grow up, and in time watched his children grow up, including one named Lewis, of whom she was particularly fond.

She was saddened to learn of Lewis's divorce, but, after my own divorce, the obvious came to her mind. Lewis and I should have married each other in the first place, but we didn't. And then, with us both single once again, there was another chance.

I was 29 by then, and Mom didn't need a spinster daughter hanging around all her life, so she arranged things between Lewis and me.

And she was right. By then I had gotten over my distaste for men, and my innate concupiscent inclinations were suggesting that it was time to try again. Lewis came into my life at just the right time. He was everything my first husband was not: Lewis was thoughtful and considerate, knowledgeable and wise, serious but witty. "I could fall for him," I thought, when Mom started bringing him over for dinner sometimes. In fact, I did just that; I did fall for him. It was destined.

We were married on my 31st birthday. He was a little older than I, and wore a little goatee that made him look even older. I didn't like it much, but married him anyway. He kindly shaved it off to celebrate the occasion.

Mom was delighted; I think she loved Lewis almost as much as I did. To prove it, she gave him as a wedding present a cute little painting by a fellow named Norman Rockwell, who had lived near friends of hers in Arlington, Vermont, and later in Stockbridge, Massachusetts. The painting was called "Second Street," and portrayed a scene right there in Stockbridge, just across the tracks. She had bought it cheaply, she told me, when Rockwell was still unknown, and long before the Rockwell Museum was founded, which in recent decades has driven up the prices of his paintings to such ridiculously high levels, into the millions of dollars.

Lewis fell in love with the painting, just as he had fallen in love with me, and treasured it, just as he treasured me. Yes, he treasured me, and maybe money too, because a few years later, when Rockwell started getting famous, Lewis became almost fanatical, watching the sale prices on other Rockwell paintings shoot up, treasuring and coveting "Second Street," as he sedulously re-estimated its rising

147

value from time to time. "And I have an original Rockwell!" thought Lewis proudly. Said Lewis proudly. Proclaimed Lewis proudly.

I didn't like his bragging mood, but I kept on loving him anyway. He really is a dear man, and I always love just being close to him, even when we aren't doing anything.

The years went by. We lived most of our life at New Milford, on the Sound, while Lewis was teaching math in New Haven. Finally, when the time came to retire, we both thought of western Massachusetts, where we had spent vacations and visits in the Berkshires. We loved Stockbridge, the very town that Lewis's beloved Rockwell painting depicted. So that is where we bought our retirement home.

That was seven years ago, and we have been very happy here ever since. But it all came to an end two years ago when we came back from a weekend visit to Lake George, and saw what had happened to our house.

* * * * *

We filled out all the required police reports and insurance forms, but the total number of things stolen was but a small fraction of the total number of our household goods, and the insurance benefits we received through our one-million-dollar general household policy were a proportionately small fraction. Our valuable Rockwell painting carried the only individual coverage, which amounted to the $2,500 my mother had paid for it "way back when," even though we knew, and especially Lewis knew, that it must be worth many times that now, perhaps in the millions of dollars, to hear him tell it.

I was sorry to see that Lewis was so deeply distressed and distraught as he focused on the loss of his painting. Sure it was a tragedy, but he seemed to be overdoing it, although I confess I did like the painting too. It was very characteristic of Rockwell's early years, typical of his interest and focus on small town America, with its almost cartoon style of presenting ordinary people, simply and unadorned, in their everyday life. Second Street was the somewhat poorer backside of the rather well-to-do front and face of Stockbridge.

But for Lewis, unfortunately, it was more than that: it was the money. Lewis was obsessed with how much the painting must now be worth. He watched auction prices of paintings on the internet, all over the country, especially Rockwell paintings, of course. Hardly a day went by without his announcing at the breakfast table, or the supper table, that such-and-such a painting of Normal Rockwell's just sold for 2 million dollars, or 3.2 million dollars, "and it's not half as good as ours. We've just lost two million dollars." And then a little while later it would be, "We've just lost three point two million dollars." I thought of telling him that if we lost two million dollars yesterday, we could have lost only one point two million today, but I didn't think that would help, so I didn't say anything. Then there was another painting that sold for $8.45 million. I think it was a record, although some of Rockwell's paintings, like Picasso's and Lichtenstein's, are selling for millions more than that now. Anyway, Lewis somehow figured that "Second Street" had to be worth $6,000,000 and that's what stuck in his mind and in his craw.

* * * * *

I was slow to recover from the shock and horror of the burglary, but Lewis never did recover from it. Not for a long time. His lamentations and jeremiads went on nonstop.

He was overcome by a weighty torpidity and a persistent hebetude. He was making himself sick. He was making me sick. His brow took on a permanent ugly frown. His jaw trembled. He lost weight. He had headaches. A suffocating inanition permeated his entire body, his very life. He had trouble sleeping. He kept me awake. He had nightmares. When he did go to sleep he talked in it. Talked nonsense. Unintelligible, unhappy talk.

"Lewis," I said, "this is not the end of the world. You mustn't let this one calamity ruin the rest of our lives."

"My life is already ruined. How can I go on, bobbing along, with a happy smile on my face when I have lost six million dollars in the damn robbery?"

"But Lewis," I would say, "You don't know that it would be worth six million, and besides, you didn't lose anything, because it didn't cost you anything. It was a gift, remember?"

"I lost six million," he insisted.

"We still have each other," I tried to comfort him.

I needed some help. I needed some advice. Lewis needed some help. Lewis needed some advice. I knew that. Professional help. Help in his head. Psychiatric help. But I knew he would never go to a psychiatrist or anybody like that. So I went. I went to Doctor Himmelfarb.

It didn't take Himmelfarb and me long to realize what we had to do. I think we both saw it at the same time. "Oh, Doctor, thanks. I agree, and I'll do it." So I paid him his exorbitant fee and went to see my aging (92) mother and told her what I was doing. Then I waited for a relatively calm moment when I was alone with Lewis.

"Darling," I said gently one evening after supper, when he had had a couple of drinks and seemed relaively relaxed, "Darling, I went over to see Mother this afternoon."

"Yes, that's nice. And how is she?"

"She seemed all right, I guess . . . I don't think she's going to live much longer."

"Nobody lives forever. Sometimes I wish I were dead too."

"Oh, Darling, don't say that! What would I ever do without you?"

"So, what did your mother have to say this time? She is a sweet lady. I've always loved her, you know."

"She dropped a bomb."

"A bomb? What are you talking about?"

"A bomb. About the painting. About Second Street."

"Yes, what?"

"She said she didn't want to tell you, because she didn't want to upset you."

"Tell me what?"

"About the painting. Lewis, the painting was fake. It wasn't by Norman Rockwell at all. It was a nice painting anyway, and it was painted by a good artist, but it wasn't Rockwell. He faked it, and signed Rockwell's name. Mom thought it was real when she bought it, but, by the time she learned it was fake, so many of her friends and family liked it that she saw no need to tell the truth about it."

"Oh my God!" said Lewis, at a loss for words to adequately express his surprise and astonishment. "Are you sure? How can this be?" he finally babbled in disbelief. "My precious Rockwell? Not a Rockwell? Then it's not worth much. Maybe not even one million. Do you think it's worth a thousand?" he bleated in disbelief. "How about a hundred and twenty-five dollars for the frame?" sarcastically letting out his sudden fury.

"Holy Cow!" he went on, sounding dazed and baffled. "How could she do this to me?"

"She hasn't done anything to you," I tried to soothe him. "You're doing it to yourself. It was never worth much, and you haven't lost much. Nothing, really. And you still have me, remember?" I said once more, as I took him by the arms and tenderly kissed his cheek as romantically as I could, under the circumstances.

Then, for a while, silence. He didn't have anything to say, and I had already said what I had to say.

So we quietly had another little drink and went to bed early. Lewis gradually relaxed. He even went off to sleep before he could tell me goodnight one last time, and the next morning he looked like a different person. His facial muscles had softened, and he wasn't frowning as he had been doing since the robbery. His voice sounded almost jolly as he said, "Hey, I'll fry the bacon and eggs if you'll make the toast and coffee."

After breakfast we were both calm and relaxed, but felt an underlying tiredness from the tension of the evening before. So we decided it was time for a morning nap.

Lewis's recovery from his pathological depression was remarkable. Almost immediately he was his old, former self, outgoing, gregarious, chatty, witty, entertaining, loveable. He never mentioned the painting again, not for a long while . . . And I certainly didn't. He gained back the weight he had lost, and directed more attention to me.

About seven months later a remarkable thing happened. The painting was found.

It turned up in a pawn shop in Pittsfield, which is not far from Stockbridge, where it had been painted originally.

153

There was a court case involving the matter of the pawn broker's receiving stolen goods, but fortunately Lewis and I didn't have to get too involved in that, beyond "providing positive identification" of the painting. In due course, we were able to get the painting back, after delays for the court proceedings and payment of minor administrative fees, etc.

Neither of us felt like looking at it, as we had done in the past. The sight of it brought no joy, and the painting was remanded to the attic with the useless CD's and VCR's to join our lovely old RCA Victor 78 RPM hand-crank phonograph, known as "The Victrola," stored there in desuetude.

I thought that would be the end of the story. However, a year or two later, when Lewis had gotten bitten by a Spring Cleaning bug, he brought the painting down from the attic with some other junk, and said, "Let's get rid of some of this stuff; it's not doing any good up there, collecting dust and spider webs."

"All right," I said, "I'll take it to the Salvation Army or Goodwill. Somebody might like to have it." Lewis agreed.

So when he was out playing golf the next day, with his spirits and health now almost fully recovered from the frightful months of depression and distress, I took the painting to the Salvation Army. They were a little confused by what I insisted upon, but they agreed because it meant a small bit of easy money for them. I had them give me a receipt for the donation, describing the painting briefly (Street Scene, they called it) with size and date and estimated value ($150).

I then told them I wanted to buy the painting back "for a friend," and paying them $150 in cash. I wanted to be sure to cover my ploy in case it ever were examined. They were delighted, although they thought I was a bit nuts. I had them put the painting in another old box and took it out to the car, where I clearly marked it, "Personal items belonging to Jennifer Gallagher. Please do not disturb until called for." (Jennifer is our married daughter.) I figured my husband would never open that.

You see, the painting was real. It was on the advice of the psychiatrist that my mother and I had cooked up the story of it's being fake in order to save my dear husband from the pecuniary obsession that was driving him crazy. But, Goodness! I couldn't just do nothing, even if we hadn't done anything to earn it. I couldn't throw away something worth six million dollars, even me, with my disdain for money and distaste for the over-pricing of modern paintings, in spite of the misery and unhappiness it had brought to my dear Lewis and me. I took the box back to the attic and put it in a far corner that we had cleaned out. No need to clean out there again for another twenty years.

If he should ever find the painting again, I don't know what I would do. If I didn't tell the truth, but stuck with the story and made him believe it was worthless, we could lose $6,000,000. If I did tell him the truth, he would be obsessed again with idea of owning a real Rockwell, and could lose his mind again, and this time probably take mine with it.

Oh my! What a Hobson's choice! I hope I don't ever have to face that: the sanity of my loving husband or six

155

million dollars? That's worse than "The Lady or the Tiger."

Well, I didn't have to worry about that now. I knew Lewis wouldn't be going back up in the attic anytime soon, and in due course I would get the thing over to Jennifer. I could relax now. Relax and enjoy my dear Lewis, my new Lewis who was once again his old self.

It was only two weeks after that eventful Saturday that there came another eventful Saturday. I was out getting my hair done at the salon as I like to do every month or so, and Lewis was out playing golf again. He was still out when I came home, and he didn't get back until almost suppertime, much later than his usual. He had a big grin on his face as I came in. "How was the golf?" I asked, already knowing it must have gone rather well to account for his smile.

"I was hitting the ball quite well for a change, but my putting hasn't been so hot lately, since about the time I got my new clubs for my birthday. I never liked my new putter much, so I decided to try to find my old one. I thought I had seen it in the attic when were cleaning out up there a while ago, so I just went up there and found it. It feels pretty good, and I'm gonna use it the next time I play."

I felt a little shudder as I heard the words "up in the attic." What would have happened if he had seen the box with the painting in it? So of course I didn't say anything. I didn't need to. He went on: "And a funny thing must have happened. I saw an old box of Jennifer's things that we must have missed when we were cleaning out. Apparently it had gotten mixed up with some old clothes of hers that we were supposed to throw away, for it still had the old fake picture of Second Street in it. You know, that thing that had been making me sick all the time. I couldn't stand the thought of having it in the same house with us, so right away I took it in for donation as we had planned to do in the first place. But here's my old putter, see? An oldie but goodie. I wish I had had it with me on the course today. I'll bet it could have saved me four or five strokes. But I'll use it next time."

I was stunned. I had to keep a sweet smile pasted on my face as the surprise and shock raced all over my body, inside and out. I could only think of hurrying to the Salvation Army immediately, but alas, it was after seven by then, and they would be closed anyway. Besides, what would I tell Lewis? I would do it tomorrow. Oh, darn! Tomorrow's Sunday; they'll be closed. Well, that means they won't have any customers either. I'll do it first thing Monday.

What a weekend that was for me, trying to keep a smile to match my dear husband's rejuvenated happy state while I was desperately picturing six million dollars fluttering away. I couldn't wait for Monday to come; I mostly stayed awake waiting for it.

When Monday finally came, I gave Lewis some excuse and rushed out right after a quick cup of coffee for breakfast.

Once again the Salvation Army people thought I was nuts. And I was beginning to wonder too. They knew nothing about the painting since I had brought it in to donate it, and then, strangely they thought, bought it back "for your friend, you said." No they had not seen it since then. No one had brought it back to the Salvation Army. Strange. I couldn't figure it, so I went home and tried to think. I couldn't say anything to Lewis of course, or that would give away the whole thing.

About midnight, between nightmares, it hit me. "Maybe he took it to Goodwill," I thought. We often used the terms Salvation Army and Goodwill almost interchangeably. "I'll bet that's what he did. I'll go to Goodwill and get it the first thing tomorrow."

So I did. "Oh yes," the Goodwill lady said with a smile, relieving my distraught self like you wouldn't believe. "He was such a nice gentleman, and the piece looked fancier than most of the home-made paintings we get here that nobody wants. We even sold it the very same afternoon. Got $200 for it. Probably should have asked for $300, it sold so quick."

I was stunned. "Do you know who bought it? Can you give me a name, or a phone number, or an address, or anything?" I was at the end of my wits. "There's been a terrible mistake."

"Oh, I'm sorry. We don't normally record the names of our customers -- the people who make the purchases -- only the donors. For tax purposes, you know. I think I could tell you who donated it though . . . I have it here somewhere . . .

I didn't wait to hear any more, but staggered out without even thanking the nice lady for handling the matter. Now what? I thought of going to Mother's, like I did when my first husband told me he wanted a divorce, but now that was probably the last place I should go to, and besides it was too early, only a little after eight. Any bars open now? I wondered. I could use a drink. I would have to think of something to tell Lewis as to why I had to rush out so early. Perhaps to walk the dog -- but we don't have a dog.

I didn't feel very good. Six million dollars lost? Then as the ensuing days passed, I didn't feel any better. It just got worse. Bad.

I was overcome by a weighty torpidity and a persistent hebetude. I was making myself sick. I was making my husband sick. My brow took on a permanent ugly frown. My jaw trembled. I lost weight. I had headaches. A suffocating inanition permeated my entire body, my very life. I had trouble sleeping. I kept Lewis awake. I had nightmares. When I did go to sleep I talked in it. Talked nonsense. Unintelligible, unhappy talk.

THE END

So-called Racism

Racism may be more widely spread than most people realize. There may even be racism next-door to you. Or maybe even IN-doors where you live. Take my grandfather, for instance.

* * * * *

My grandfather was an English teacher. At least he was once an English teacher, back before I ever knew him, and that was before he got religion and went into the ministry. Why he made that switch is quite a story in itself, but that's another story.

Anyway, Granddad's love of English never left him -- his love of English literature and English grammar and English word usage. Grandfather was the only person I ever knew who would say, "It is I" instead of "I's me," if someone said, "Who's there?" And he would say, "Whom did you play with this afternoon?" Things like that. I loved him anyway, and I knew he was right of course, but the other kids sort of laughed him off or didn't pay any attention to his linguistic niceties.

Granddad also frowned at our increasingly frequent use of expressions like "awesome," and "super," and "outta sight."/1 That was before "cool" became the popular word. He told us that when he was young the adjectives in vogue were "swell," and "keen," and "neat," words now long since obsolete. We laughed at him, or with him, but loved him anyway.

161

Fortunately -- fortunately for him anyway -- Granddad died before "unbelievable" and "incredible" rampaged through our language like the plague or a cancer virus. He would have moaned and groaned to hear important people in all walks of life filling every possible lacuna in their speech with these meaningless words:

"The enemy mortar fire was incredible (their aim was so bad none of us got a scratch)."

"Last year's Derby was unbelievable (the winning time was seven and a half seconds off the track record, the worst time in forty-seven years)."

"The weekend blizzard was incredible (it left only half an inch of snow when we expected a foot)."

Things like that. But my father, who incidentally had gone into the ministry just like Granddad, also would talk about what he called "buzz words," or unconscious "verbal ticks," that had no place in proper English but were peppering the language. He sort of picked up Granddad's banner, or mantle, and tried to get us kids to quit saying "like" for no reason at all, as the sportscasters and TV news commentators and politicians and VIP's used to do all the time. Almost all of them did it.

And now it's hard for us kids not to say "ya know" every few seconds because we hear all these other people, important grown-ups, doing it all the time. I know

---

/1 I have often wondered whether our expression "outta sight" came from German *ausgezeichnet.* They sound rather similar, and mean about the same thing, if they have any meaning at all.

Granddad would be boiling over in his grave to hear the way people talk today, and I'm sorry. But, ya know, I can't help it.

So every generation has brought its buzzwords into the language. A few years ago I heard someone on TV talk about a "so-called terrorist," or something like that. Then it was a so-called hero. (John McCain, I think they were talking about.) "So-called" seemed like a neat expression to me, one that wasn't pushy but sounded as though you were not exactly sure of something, or one that could mean or demean almost anything you wanted it to mean or demean. I tried it out on my cousin's French poodle, all trimmed and primmed with ribbons for a dog show, and referred to her as a "so-called" dog or a so-called poodle. So-called poodle I guess I said. That comment brought great laughter, and before long we were saying "so-called" all around the house, and all around school, and all around the neighborhood, as though it meant something, which of course it didn't. At school we suddenly had so-called compositions and a so-called study hall and so-called erasers and a so-called cafeteria and a so-called principal. At first it was just kind of a joke, but everybody caught on, like a common denominator sort of thing, and we began saying so-called this and so-called that and so-called schoolhouse and so-called teachers and so-called books without even thinking about it.

* * * * *

163

We live in Alabama, so we have some Blacks at our high school. So-called Blacks anyway. I've heard that there are some so-called Blacks in some other states too, and that so-called Blacks there are even allowed to vote when they get old enough, and are beginning to do a lot of other things that so-called white people were already allowed to do.

But just because you MAY do something doesn't always mean you CAN do it. I always liked to run. In our backyard touch football games I was one of the fastest kids on the block, but when we got to high school it was different. I was the second fasted white boy in my class, but there were at least four so-called Black boys who could beat our pants off in the hundred-yard dash. In basketball it was the same way. The so-called Black boys were quicker, had longer arms, and could jump higher than any of us so-called white boys.

As far as sports were concerned, I did best in football, because I had a high so-called IQ. That's what they said, the School Guidance Counselor and our so-called football coach. The coach made me a quarterback, because quarterbacks, so-called quarterbacks anyway, were supposed to be smart or able to make quick decisions.

My so-called father was pretty proud of me I guess, but I worked hard at football practice and got knocked down a lot. However, I always got up again and I thought he should have been more proud of me than he actually was. "You're smart," he explained, "naturally you would be made quarterback." He explained that white boys in general are smarter than Black boys and have statistically higher IQ's, and that "a quarterback has to be smart and

164

think fast. Look at the NFL for instance," he said. "Ninety per cent of the players are Black because they are stronger than whites, and ninety per cent of the quarterbacks are white because they are smarter than Blacks."

"That sounds like so-called Racism, Dad."

"You don't have to be a so-called Racist to see that there are differences between the races besides the color of their skin," he said. "Let me tell you a few things." And with that he started in to give me a sermon that lasted almost three days.

* * * * *

"The Bible tells us that God created Heaven and Earth, and then everything ON Earth, and then created man, like Adam and Eve. But you must realize that all that is merely symbolic and beautiful, like poetry. All God really did was to create Nature, but that alone was quite a feat, with all its mysterious forces and atoms and molecules and neutrinos having the potential to combine and evolve into all sorts of plants and animals and so-called Man. And that's what happened. What COULD happen DID happen, under God's watchful eye, of course. Noah's sons Shem and Ham represent the two main stems of Mankind."

Because Dad had studied science and anthropology before he went into the ministry, he was always preaching that the Bible should not be taken literally. "You shouldn't take an eye for an eye and a tooth for a tooth, but give and take love instead. That's why love is a matter of give and take," Dad would say with a chuckle.

165

And then Dad explained what a beautiful thing God's design of so-called Evolution was -- different kinds of plants and animals, different classes and orders of jellyfish and insects and frogs and mammals, always making new species. God sat back and watched it all evolve, more or less as he had planned. There were different kinds of felines -- tiger-cats and bob-cats and pole-cats and even so-called tom-cats. And different kinds of apes -- monkeys and gorillas and chimpanzees, each with special features and abilities different from the others, and Early Man, who back then still looked a lot like his cousins, the apes. Shem went to Africa and founded the African race, and Ham went to the Caucasus and founded the Caucasian race. Shem's family became the Ulotrichi Negroes, and Ham's family the Leiotrichi Caucasians.

And human beings evolved too, Dad explained, and these different groups of human beings evolved with different strengths and abilities, just like animals did. Some of these differences you might say were good, and maybe some not so good. Monkeys were good at climbing trees and culling each other for so-called fleas, but antelopes could run faster, with their long legs and hooves. Would you want to put long legs and hooves on a so-called monkey?

Dad would say it's the same idea between different so-called races. Blacks are better than whites at some things, generally speaking, and whites are better than so-called Blacks at some things, generally speaking. This is represented in the Scriptures. We can turn to the Bible for the image and explanation of how God works and how things came about.

166

"You should always turn to the Bible to see how the will of God and the Word of God pervade all these ideas," Dad said, "but it is clear that God wanted variety on the Earth, and that he wanted the races to be different."

"I don't think the races are all that different, except for skin color," I said.

"Oh yes they are! And if Man had not stepped in with modern devices of transportation and communication, which serve to mix the races, it would have worked out more like what God planned. God expected the white and Black races to become separate species like the Denisovans and Neanderthals and the Cro-Magnons. It was a slow evolutionary process and it only got halfway along before technology stepped in and started messing up the Plan."

"What do you mean, Dad? Do you think God wanted the races to be different?"

"Of course He did. Take a look at them. Each race has its own abilities and differences, and not just skin."

"Well, I guess Blacks are stronger and more athletic; is that what you mean? In general terms, of course."

"Sure, that's part of it. That's what I'm saying. Also their arms are an average of two inches longer and their bones are stronger, especially their jawbones and skulls. That's why the so-called boxing champions are all Black with rare exceptions. Whites are weaker because they evolved living indoors where you had to have a so-called house. They had to stay inside in the winter because it was

167

cold, so they spent their time reading and studying and exercising their so-called brains. Meanwhile the Blacks in Africa could exercise their bodies and just run around outside and play ball and throw javelins all year long. After a few dozen millennia these things begin to tell."

"Gosh Dad, does the so-called Bible say all that?"

"Don't call the Bible 'so-called'."

"Sorry Dad. 'So-called' doesn't mean anything. It's just an expression, like 'Ya know.' Saying 'Ya know?' doesn't mean you expect anybody to know anything. Ya know what I'm saying?"

"I think so; thank you for the clarification. But, in answer to your question: No, the Bible doesn't exactly say all that, but that is what it means. It means that God wanted His different races or peoples to develop all sorts of different characteristics and possibilities. And also talents and skills. And it's why God gets upset when He sees people trying to destroy the progress He had already made in developing these different racial characteristics and abilities."

"Trying to destroy them? Really? What do you mean?"

"It goes right against God's plan for developing human abilities, this mixing of the races. Abraham Lincoln, who was like a God to many of us here on Earth, saw it. He said, 'I am not, nor ever have been, in favor of Negroes . . . to intermarry with white people.'/2 Mixing the races, or so-called miscegenation, as Lincoln and others have called it, erodes and weakens the individual talents and salient characteristics of the different races. I have to agree with Lincoln in a way. I think that love between the races is a wonderful thing wherever it exists, and love between a white person and a so-called Black person is to be commended and applauded. We should love everybody, the Bible says. Even living together, or co-habitation, may be acceptable in certain cases, if there is true love. But that does not have to mean marriage and certainly not children. Children of these associations may grow up with split personalities and feelings of isolation from either society, not to mention loss of the pure and distinct human traits that God wants each race or species eventually to have."/3

"Gee Dad, this is fascinating. I didn't know all that . . . But Dad?"

"Yes?"

"There's something you ought to know too."

"And what is that?"

"Do you know who my sister wants . . . I mean, WHOM my sister wants . . . to marry?"

/2 Lincoln-Douglas Debates, 1858

/3 See *Square Peg in a Round Hole*, by Hayward Inabinett, the serious autobiography of a man who did not know whether he was Black or white.

"She can marry anyone she wants to."

"Did you know he is a so-called Black?"

"Black? No!" he exploded, his face bursting out red as a ripe tomato. "No, of course I didn't know it. And I can't believe she would want to do that."

"Well, she does, and you said she could marry anyone she wanted to."

"I meant any white boy. She knows that."

"No, she doesn't. She wants to marry this one. So what are you going to do? Are you going to let her?"

Dad thought a while before replying.

"I don't know that I could stop her. But if she does want to marry this fellow, she will have to promise that she will never sleep with him."

"Never sleep with him?"

"Or else he will have to promise to use so-called protection," he thundered.

THE END

The Gentleman

History tells us that there were several *Ducs de Richlieu.* The one I have in mind was Louis. He was a Duc de Richlieu, a grand-nephew of the famous one, the Cardinal, but he was also a "gentleman."

There were many other Louis's in France in those days, and some of them were kings and dukes, and a few were gentlemen as well, so to speak.

This Louis Duc de Richlieu lived in a nice country place where he could hunt and fish and ride horseback with his friendly neighbor and competitor, the Duc de Bourgogne, and other friends, and do most other things that gentlemen and aristocrats like to do if they can afford it. Louis also had a lovely wife, Marguerite, who was also very energetic; in fact she was even more energetic in some ways than Louis himself was.

Now to make the story interesting, another character must be involved, namely, the stable-boy. Some of the stable-boys in France in those days were quite good looking, and often young and energetic as well. But now we should get on with our story, which is to give an example of what it meant to be a "gentleman."

Once when Louis was out on an all-day ride with his equestrian friends, Marguerite's boredom and hormonal energy combined to lead her into some early afternoon

171

activities that were somewhat beyond the limits of her ladyship's normal, and proper, social behavior.

It so happened that the aforementioned stable-boy also had some afternoon time on his hands that day. He had finished most of his daily chores, having saddled up the early-morning horses, fed the other animals, cleaned out the stable, hung up the fly paper, and washed out the milk cans. Ever concerned for the well-being and comfort of his employers, he came to the Lady of the House, who was strolling in the garden with nothing better to do, and ask her whether she could use his services in any way.

As it was a bright sunny day, she pondered the question for a couple of seconds, took another look at his firm youthful body, and gently replied, "Well yes, perhaps there is, thank you very much."

* * * * *

Now in accordance with the reader's expectation, the Duke returned from his ride earlier than planned. He entered his wife's bedroom and, to his considerable astonishment/1 and to her considerable surprise/1 found another man in there with her. The man looked like the stable-boy. It *was* the stable-boy. Well, better the stable-boy than the Duc de Bourgogne, who could have been a real threat.

/1 This story may derive in part from one of Professor Ruge's English lessons at St Albans School many years ago, about Noah Webster. According to Mr. Ruge, the roles were reversed: it was Noah Webster's wife that returned

172

"Madame," said Louis (he called her Madame on formal occasions), "Madame, think of how embarrassing it would have been to you if anyone but me had come in here at a time like this." And with that he bowed (slightly) and withdrew.

THE END

Epilogue

Of course the stable-boy also withdrew, and promptly left the Lady's quarters.

THE FINAL END

---

home unexpectedly early from shopping one afternoon and found Noah and the chambermaid together in the bedroom, *in flagrante delicto*.

"Noah!" asseverated Mrs. Webster rather forcefully, "I'm surprised!"

"No, my dear," gently replied Noah, foremost grammarian that he was -- "you're *astonished*. *We're* surprised."

Short Stories at Last

Happy Girl

Different people measure success and happiness in different ways. For some people, happiness depends on how much you are getting paid on your job, or how much money you have already stowed away. For others, health and physical well-being are the important things. Still others view religion and godliness as the only path to true happiness. Some consider themselves successful and happy simply when they are able to help people and bring success or happiness or comfort to others.

Crysalle Baltimore was a happy and successful young woman. At least she thought she was. She was 24 years old, quite nice looking, some might say stylish, even prepossessing. She had a job that she enjoyed, a job that gave her quite a good income, especially considering her age and education level. She had studied at a community college for a while but dropped out the middle of her sophomore year.

Life was not always so rosy for Crysalle. As a child she grew up in a household where her parents were arguing much of the time, if not actually fighting. They would take turns hugging and spanking Crysalle, and then go back to their own squabbles. Crysalle felt that she was at least partly the cause of her parents' altercations. Specialists say children often feel they are to blame when there is discord in the family. When Crysalle was ten years old, her parents, Ezekiel and Cora, got married. Until that time, they had lived, unbeknownst to Crysalle, out of wedlock. Even back then that was not so unusual among lower-middle-class couples like Dora and Ezekiel.

It was about that time that many states were abolishing their outdated laws restricting racially mixed marriages, or miscegenation, as Abraham Lincoln and others called it. You see, Crysalle's mother, Cora, was white, and her father, Ezekiel, was Black. Like more and more people nowadays, particularly women, Cora took pity on the Blacks in this country, and felt remorse and even guilt over the way white people looked down on Black people, and the way they had owned Black slaves that had been brought over from Africa, often against their will.

Cora decided to devote her adult life to the care and betterment of the Blacks, or Negroes and Coloreds, as they were called then. She worked energetically for the NAACP and the National Urban League, but that was not enough. The Black race had suffered more under years of slavery and discrimination than many people realized, and serious atonement was due.

Like some other sympathetic white women have been doing in recent decades, Cora thereupon decided to "befriended" a Black man, to help atone for the conditions of thralldom that his race had endured as slaves, and later as second-class citizens who were discriminated against in this supposedly free and democratic country. She wanted to prove that Blacks were persons just like anybody else. It did not bother her that probably only a little, perhaps none, of her man's black blood came from pre-Civil War African-American slaves./1

176

Accordingly, she gave herself to Ezekiel Baltimore, a day worker whose father had been one of the janitors at Cora's high school. It was the least she could do -- and also the most -- thought kindhearted Cora, with her idealism and compassion. But that was not enough. Ultimately she had to marry Ezekiel to prove to herself and the world that she was serious about it.

Ezekiel, like almost all the people we call Blacks and Negroes in the United States, then and now, was not pure Black, perhaps not even half Black. But that was enough, far more than enough, to qualify him as a Black person in most places. In America there has been racial mixing going on ever since 1607, when Jamestown was first settled. Integration, or amalgamation, has proceeded apace, inexorably, over these few centuries, especially since the Civil War, in spite of fitful opposition movements and intermittent unconstitutional "Jim Crow" laws and such practices separating the races, plus the lingering social stigma of miscegenation and couplings between Blacks and white people that still remains in some places to the present day.

Look at the great mulatto race that has now spread across almost the entire United States, even touching the borders of Vermont and Minnesota. Look at all the wonderful athletes and other great men who have been mulattoes:

/1 Since 1880 some 3,250,000 Black Africans have immigrated to the United States. This is over ten times the total of between 280,000 and 300,000 Black African slaves that were brought over between 1607 and 1861. (Source, Wikipedia)

Magic Johnson, O.J. Simpson, Clarence Thomas, Jackie Robinson, Sidney Poitier, Booker T. Washington, Louis Armstrong, Bill Cosby, and even more. We call them Blacks, but they are not really black anymore, and many, if not most, of them have more white blood than black blood. Even Tiger Woods is only one quarter Black, if that. Mulatto means a mix of Black and white, although you don't hear the word used much nowadays. The great mulatto race was founded by our white and Black ancestors through their love affairs, escapades, and joint activities, whether they were legal or illegal, open or clandestine./2

Ezekiel Baltimore was approximately a Quadroon, that is, a person who has one quarter Black blood and three quarters white. His skin was very dark, however, considerably darker than that of most Quadroons./3

/2 See WE LOVE EACH OTHER – SORTA, in *Short Stories for Pleasure* by Daniel Hoyt Daniels (2019)

/3 It is rare, but some Quadroons and Octaroons are so light that, only judging by their skin, you would almost think they were white, except for other features like bone structure and muscle formation and hair material. Although most people may not know it, many geneticists some decades ago classified the human species into two principal divisions, simply depending on characteristics of hair, i.e. whether kinky or straight, that is to say, ulotrichi or leiotrichi. These features are determined by the shape of the cross section of a hair, whether circular and tubular, or oval and flat.

I once asked my step-mother why it was that the child of black and white parents was always Black. Her naive answer, which I have never been able to improve upon, was "because black blood is stronger."

Well, generally speaking, the strongest people today are the Blacks, which is to say, Mulattoes, in almost every case. Look at our boxers, and our football players, and our basketball players, for instance. And Zeke certainly was stronger than Cora -- not just because he was a man, and not just physically, but emotionally, psychologically, and maybe even spiritually as well. He bossed her around, told her what she could do and could not do. He practically made her his slave./4

Cora bore her chosen onus dutifully through the years. It was her personal atonement for the sins of all slave-holding white masters over the past centuries.

Little Crysalle, now an Octaroon, happened to have very light skin, even for an Octaroon. Some Octaroons can be quite dark, although never really black. Different Octaroon siblings often have several different shades of skin color, even if they are from the same father. It cannot be predicted. There are cases of "throw-backs," or "*tornatrás*," as they are known as in Mexico, in which the specific characteristics of one ancestor can become prominently manifest even three or four generations later.

* * * * *

/4 In 1798 Virginia passed a law making it illegal for Black people to own white people as slaves. (Wikipedia)

Crysalle wasn't particularly conscious of race until she started school. On the playground at her "integrated" elementary school, the white children still naturally flocked together and the Blacks together. Poor Crysalle did not know whether to zig or to zag. At first, everyone thought she was white because of her white skin and her pretty face. Then someone commented on her somewhat thicker, full lips and her somewhat wider nose, and in the heartless way that children have, unthinkingly announced, "She's Black! Look at her, she's Black!" They looked closer. It was true. From then on, everyone in that school knew she was Black.

Thereafter Crysalle's high-school years were a torment. She sought sympathy and guidance from her parents, but got none from her father and very little from her mother. Her teachers and school authorities accused her of being a trouble maker and told her to behave and stop acting uppity. Crysalle was a misfit. She didn't know whether she was Black or white./5

She withdrew into a taciturn, morose shell. She wanted to leave this school and leave this horrible town and go to the Big City and get a job as a waitress or shoe-shine girl or something -- anything. Her parents of course refused to contemplate such an idea and said they would get the police after her unless she behaved. "You must at least wait until you finish high school," said her mother. Neither

---

/5 See *Square Peg in a Round Hole,* by Hayward Inabinett, the serious autobiography of a man who did not know whether he was Black or white.

Cora nor Zeke ever finished high school, but Crysalle agreed to stay and work toward a GED, for she knew how important it was to get a good education.

Zeke never forgave Crysalle for wanting to be white, like her mother, or for wanting to pass for white. "Black isn't good enough for you? I'm not good enough for you!" he shouted furiously. Cora explained he was that way because whites had held Blacks in forced servitude in the United States of America "back before any of us were born" -- she added, to stress how serious it was.

Anyway, Crysalle toughed it out until she got her degree, and then, as soon as possible, she said *adiós* and took off for the City. Fortunately she had an older cousin there, who was married to a successful bus driver. Colenna was her name, and she let Crysalle stay and sleep on the couch until she could get a job and find a place of her own.

* * * * *

All that was four years ago.

Crysalle Baltimore is now a mature woman, almost twenty-four years old. Like her mother at that age, she is unmarried and no longer a virgin. However, unlike her mother, she has no sense of shame or embarrassment or need for atonement to anyone, Black or white. Also, unlike her mother, and unlike her father as well, Crysalle has made a financially successful career for herself, drawing upon her innate talents and abilities. Crysalle now has pride and self respect, something her mother never had. She doesn't feel she has any ancestral debts that she should

181

pay off by giving herself, or her body, to a Black man, Negro, Colored man, African American, Spade, Coon, Darkie, Jig, Jigaboo, or knowingly to a Mulatto, or to anybody else, even a white man, not of her own choosing. "Of her own choosing" was the key phrase for Crysalle.

Crysalle was able to pass for white in the Big City. It is true that she used an Afro-Skin Creamette from Zhuotop or Aichun trying to lighten her skin color somewhat more, although she hardly needed it, and she practiced pursing her lips so they didn't look quite so thick. She went to a community college with a night school and night classes to work on her pronunciation of the white English language, to eliminate any traces of her Black father's influence. She no longer said "wif" for "with," or "aks" for "ask" -- sure giveaways. Yes, and Crysalle even looked down on Blacks now. Her father had never given her any reason to look up to *him*. He had never held a decent job for long, never had any money for anything nice, wasted much of what little he did have on lottery tickets, and he never gave up speaking Black English, or Gullah, or Geechee, or something that sounded like Uncle Remus, although he was married to a white woman. He thought that having a white woman for a wife was enough of an accomplishment. It made him high class and gave him status. He didn't need to accomplish anything else, except to dominate his wife and family and boss them around and practically make slaves of *them*. /4

Crysalle looked back on her life. Her mother could lead that sort of life and take that sort of abuse if she wanted to, but not Crysalle. Crysalle smiled with satisfaction as she thought back on what a good decision it had been for her to leave home when she did and start on her own career. Look at her now. She was well dressed, stood up with

182

pride, was financially well off, practically affluent, and had friends in important places in business and in the City Government, although they all were male friends. (Crysalle had no Lesbian leanings.) She gave a bit of financial support to her cousin Colenna, who had helped her when she first came to the City, and she periodically sent a tidy little sum of money to her parents -- her mother actually -- usually every three months. She even donated to the AME Church (anonymously), and to the NAACP (anonymously). Crysalle's many city friends, and anybody else who knew her, or ever saw her, would certainly realize that she was the model of a happy, well-adjusted person.

Then something happened.

When Crysalle's cousin Colenna got the news, she was shocked, astounded. "I never would have believed Crysalle could do such a thing."

You see, Crysalle's life had been going along happily, and her parents had been getting money from her happily, although they never saw her anymore. "She seems to be making quite a lot of money," thought her father. "I wonder just what sort of a job she has."

"I've wondered about that too," said Cora. "I even wondered whether she might be selling something on the side sort of, like marijuana or drugs or something . . . But I don't think we have to worry about it. It's not our business."

But Zeke began to think, something he didn't often do. "Sell something . . .?" His dirty mind ran on. "You don't

183

think . . .?" he cryptically, elliptically, said to Cora one evening.

"Think what?"

"You don't think she's selling <u>herself</u>, up there in the Big City, do you?"

"Selling herself?" Cora had to stop and think a minute to catch up on Zeke's drift. "Oh my! You mean . . .! Oh no, she would never do a thing like that."

"How can you be so sure?"

"She would tell us."

"I don't know . . ."

"We could tell; I would feel it."

"Well, I think maybe I feel something, and I would like to find out."

So they found out. It wasn't hard. Crysalle never hid her business, and was, in fact, quite proud of how well she had done and was doing. The reason she told her parents she never wanted to see them again was that she felt they had abused her, put her down, did not love her, and had not treated her fairly. Increasingly inquisitive, Zeke and Dora went ahead and contacted Cousin Colenna, who told them, "I don't think Crysalle really has a job, in the usual sense. She quit working at the Thai restaurant quite a while ago, you know. I think she has a gentleman friend, or maybe . . .

I mean, she has a gentleman friend or two who help her and like to take care of her. You must know that."

"What'er their name?"

Colenna thought to herself -- I don't think I would tell you even if I did know -- but settled for saying, "I don't know. Why don't you ask her?"

But they did persuade Colenna to tell them where Crysalle was living, and promptly went to see her. It was quite a surprise on both sides.

Crysalle could not help throwing her arms about her mother, whom she had not seen for over three years, at the same time saying, "I told you I never wanted to see you again. What are you doing here?"

Cora and Zeke were surprised and astonished, and overcome with awe, as they entered the luxurious premises of their daughter's quarters and saw how successful looking and radiant their daughter was, with her charming, well-appointed little apartment, her elegant clothes, her self assurance, and her air of prosperity and success. Even Zeke felt a stab of pride in his daughter, but forced himself to return to his naturally intolerant and critical nature.

"I knew Crysalle had it in her," said Cora joyfully, at first.

But Zeke's little head was suddenly filled with a powerful mixture of emotions. There was a tinge of admiration for the accomplishments of his daughter, as he looked around, in overweening envy of how well she had done, but it was finally capped off by nagging doubts and wonder at how she had managed to do so well. What kind of a job did she have? What was she really into? he wondered. The possible activities he was imagining were multiplying like summer flies in a shithouse.

"I am going to get to the bottom of this," he swore silently to himself. And then, out loud: "Where did you get the money to pay for all this?" he said, casting his suspicious eyes about the premises.

"I have a job."

"Yeah? What kind of a job?" he retorted, skeptically, his doubts continuing to rise.

"I provide comfort and compassion to people who need it," she replied. "It's like home care for the aged, but it's not just old people who need care and attention," Crysalle said, slowly and carefully. "I'm sorry, I have to go now; I have an important appointment. I don't know why you had to go to the trouble of coming all the way here anyway."

"We had to see you; we had to find out if you were all right," said her mother.

"I'm fine. I have to get ready to go," she said, pushing them out.

* * * * *

"What do you think?" said Zeke, walking back to their hotel.

"I think she's doing fine, like she said. Look at her."

"I mean, how do you think she is making all that money?"

"I never thought about it. It is not my business."

"Well, I'm going to make it my business to find out. I think she has gotten into the trade," said Zeke, challenged by envy of his daughter's success. She was quite clearly more successful than he himself had ever been. She was doing this to show him up. She thought that she was better than he was. He would show her. Take her down a peg or two if necessary, even if it did cost him the little supplemental income she was providing Cora and him. He was never concerned about the purity and modesty of his daughter before, but now he realized this might be something he could seize upon.

Zeke tried to consider his options; there were not many of them.

He could go to the police and tell them he believed she was engaging in illegal activities, from prostitution to drug dealing, to account for her financial success. These things he could only suspect but could not prove. He could go to her church, if she had one, and if he could find out what church it was, but that might be difficult. He could go to a professional social worker who might be able to give Crysalle some inspiration to live an upright, pure, respectable life, or he could try to get Cousin Colenna to straighten the girl out, and help steer her into a clean and righteous lifestyle. But they didn't know Colenna very

187

well, and knew very little about <u>her</u> lifestyle; maybe it was worse than Crysalle's, for all they knew.

Zeke pondered all of these ideas as much as he could, and he tried to have Cora ponder them with him. They finally decided to seek some help from some professional social worker that was being paid by the state, with possible support from Crysalle's church, if they could find it.

* * * * *

It was with some difficulty and considerable urging, supported only lukewarmly by his wife Cora, that Zeke was able to explain his concerns to a staff member at the City Office of Health and Human Services later that afternoon. "But she is over 21," they told Zeke. "She is not your dependent and not any responsibility of yours."

"But she is my *daughter*," wailed Zeke, conjuring some moisture into the corners of his eyes. "And I'm not even sure she's not breaking the law," he added tearfully.

"This is not a court of law; this is a family counseling service."

"Oh yes, I know.   That's what we need -- family counseling."

"Well all right. If your daughter is a resident of this state, bring her here on Thursday afternoon at 2:00 o'clock. You are lucky; I just happen to have a cancellation."

At noon the next day, the only time they could expect to find Crysalle at home, they went back to her apartment and surprised her again. "What do you want this time?" said Crysalle, as expected.

"We love you. We just want to know that you are all right and safe and are doing the right thing."

"I'm fine. I told you that. What does it take for you to leave me alone?"

"We want you to come with us and talk to a friend. Thursday afternoon at 2:00 o'clock. I hope you can put off any appointments that might conflict. We only need you for a couple of hours."

"What's this all about? Are you going to put me on the Dr. Phil show?"

"That wouldn't be a bad idea. But, seriously, if you will come with us and do what we ask this one time, we will never bother you again, or impact your life uninvited."

"You promise?"

"I promise"

"You swear?"

"We swear."

"All right then, I'll go this time, if you'll leave me alone after that. But I'm never doing it again."

189

* * * * *

In addition to the sympathetic social worker, Zeke and Cora -- mostly Zeke -- thought it would be a good thing if they could bring God into it too. Remembering that when Crysalle was a child she had often trotted along with them to the AME Church without complaining, Zeke said, "Maybe there's an AME church in her neighborhood in the City. Maybe she still goes to church sometimes; let's find out."

"All right," said Cora. "Can't do any harm, I guess." So they found that there was indeed an AME church only four blocks from Crysalle's apartment. They went to see the Rector, who turned out to be one Luther Morgan Brown.

Brown remembered having occasionally seen Crysalle, "a good supporter of the church, but not very active," he offered.

"I think perhaps she needs your help," said Zeke, now in his plaintive voice.

"Of course. Just tell me what you think I can do."

"Can you meet with us on Thursday afternoon, with another friend? We all need to have a talk. Crysalle needs our help and we need your suggestions and support. I am afraid she may be deviating from the strait and narrow way of the Lord and the holy path we brought her up to follow," he said slightly sanctimoniously.

"My Goodness, it does sound serious."

So Zeke told Pastor Brown a little about Crysalle's dissolute life, and how he thought she was making her money, and Brown agreed to meet with them at 2:00 p.m. Thursday at the address of the social worker they gave him. He knew the place. He had been there before.

* * * * *

At the designated hour Thursday, the three Baltimores, Zeke and Cora and Crysalle, met Mrs. Featherstone, the HHS lady, in her office. Pastor Brown, from the Twelfth Avenue AME Church, was already there, with his collar on backwards, as usual, even though it wasn't even Sunday.

After a hasty round of introductions, Mrs. Featherstone forewent further niceties and got straight to business. "What is your problem? You seem to be a competent and well-adjusted woman," she said to Crysalle.

"Problem? I don't have any problem."

"Then what are we here for?"

Zeke cut in, while catching Pastor Brown's eye: "We are concerned about Crysalle's lifestyle and we are afraid she may be hurting herself and debasing her spirit, especially her inner self.

"Oh my!" said Mrs. Featherstone, kindly showing sudden interest in the case, "That sounds serious. Let me tell you, my dear," she sweetly said to Crysalle, "I am also an ordained deacon in the City Community Church, so I am competent to help care for the spiritual as well as the corporal needs of my clients."

191

"Corporal?"

"Physical.   Physical and bodily needs, as well as emotional and spiritual."

"I don't have any needs," said Crysalle, "I already have everything I need. I only need to get my parents out of my hair and get back to work."

"Everybody has needs, my Dear, whether they know it or not.   Even our Lord Jesus Christ had needs, didn't he, Pastor Brown?" she said, looking up. "He needed to know that everybody loved both Him and God. And Mary too, of course. Do you love God, Crysalle?"

"God is all right," said Crysalle.

"All <u>right</u>?   You mean All <u>Mighty</u>!" said Mrs. Featherstone, raising her voice somewhat and managing to look a bit shocked, whether or not it was put on.

"All right, all mighty."

"She has never been too religious," explained Cora. "But she did go to church with us, sometimes, when she was young, but now she has other problems."

"What problems?" asked Mrs. Featherstone.

"God knows," said Cora. "You better ask her. I mean, ask Crysalle."

Mrs. Featherstone turned to Crysalle: "Tell me about yourself, my Dear, and tell me why you think your parents feel you have problems."

Crysalle explained that she helped a couple of gentlemen who needed help. Sometimes she had even helped old people, but sometimes she helped people who were relatively young. She wasn't prejudiced like some people she knew were.

"You say 'people.' Do you mean men?"

"Well, yes. Men are people too, aren't they?"

(Some men are beasts, thought Mrs. Featherstone.) "How do you help them?" she persisted.

Crysalle took a deep breath. She wanted to get his over with and get out of there. "I give them care and succor. I give them attention, and listen to them. Not all men just want one thing. There are sometimes other things as well. They don't always get everything they need at home, whether they're married or not. Their home life isn't my business, but I let them tell me about it anyway. They usually like to do that, and I pretend, but usually I don't even listen to it; it goes in one ear and out the other. I'll bet you do that too, right here in your own business. My business is taking care of their needs, here and now, and making them happy, here and now. I'm not a family counselor. What's wrong with that? A lot of women don't even take care of their husband's basic needs. I have learned that much. They come to me because they need me, to listen to them and help them; to help them be

193

themselves and to fill in some of the gaps in their lives. That's all." Crysalle had gotten rather worked up, so she sat back down and tried to relax a bit.

But Pastor Brown was relentless: "Are they paying you for your 'services,' as you call it?" asked Pastor Brown.

"Do people pay <u>you</u> for <u>your</u> services?" said Crysalle, beginning to feel cornered and fenced in.

"Yes, of course. I interpret God's Word for them and help to save their souls. Like Mrs. Featherstone here helps to heal people, and save families that are split apart."

"That's right, my dear," joined in Mrs. Featherstone. "You shouldn't be intimate with men or take money from them unless you are married to them. In fact, what you are doing may be illegal. If you are being intimate with men and they are paying you for it, you could be charged with prostitution and soliciting, and that's against the law. You could even be arrested."

Crysalle turned to her father, with a touch of anger and irritation in her voice. "Izzat why you brought me heah? You wanna git me 'rested now, causse I'se made sumpin outta mah life and I'se makin' mo' money'n you evva made, wif any uh yo' lil' half-time half-assed jobs you had fo' a munt ter two here en der? En as fer marriage, wha' jew evva care 'bout marriage? I was a lil' bassard fo' 'most ten years, 'til you fine-ly married Mom. Thanks a lot," said Crysalle, looking as though she were going to cry.

194

But she turned back to Mrs. Featherstone and went on: "Even effen Ah'da been a HO, it woulda been to get even with some of them rich whites. I thought it'd please my father to get back at them, 'cause dat is whut he allers wanta to do hisseff, but he ain got whut it takes to do it. All he kin do is beat on me and call me names," she said, now in tears. Zeke was furious, speechless.

"Come now, Crysalle," intertoned Mrs. Featherstone. "This is not about your parents' problems; it is about your problems."

"I don' has no problems," insisted Crysalle once again. Dey're de ones whut has de problems. De onliest problem Ah has is gittin' dem outta mah hair'n outta mah life."

Pastor Brown thought it was time for him to rejoin the fray with some more of his own imprecations. "Do you think that God will forgive you for the unholy kind of life your are leading?"

"God don' has nuttin' to do 'thit. He don' even has to know 'bout tit, less'n you goes 'n tells 'em."

"But he WILL know! He DOES know! He knows everything."

"Den He knows Ah ain' ahurtin' nobody. Ah cud jone de Army and git a gun and go Iraq and start a-killing peoples. Wud God like dat betta?"

"You are trying to change the subject."

195

"'Sides, Ah suppote His wuks. Ah contibuz to His church heah on Urt, including your AME church, Mr. Brown, even anonymously sometimes. De Bible tell us not to brag or tell ovvers 'bout how much we gives to charity and de church and doze things."

But Pastor Brown was not about to back down: "No one can buy their way into Heaven, and you are following a worthless, adulterous, peccant way of life that you should be ashamed of. You have no self-worth. You have no self-pride. The truth is that you are going to Hell, young lady."

"Pride be a sin too," murmured Crysalle, by now somewhat subdued and barely audible. "To you evertin's a sin and everbuddy's a sinner."

But Pastor Brown continued pounding. "Don't you be mocking me! I'm telling you you are a worthless sinner and there is no health in you. You are beyond hope and you are going to Hell," he proclaimed, even more vehemently this time.

Then Mrs. Featherstone piled on: "Did you hear him? You are worthless, just like he said. Your arrant impudicity and your despicable behavior are illegal, immoral, and an insult to our loving God in Heaven. And you are going to Hell," she said, confirming the Pastor's asseverations. "To Hell, do you understand?" she added in clarification and emphasis.

Crysalle looked around at all the accusing eyes and faces: Pastor Brown, Mrs. Featherstone, and her father Zeke. Even her mother, Cora, seemed to have joined the others in their frowns and judgements, disparaging and denigrating her, in unison, from every side. They all continued pouring out their accusations and jeremiads and diatribes onto Crysalle for the next fifteen or twenty minutes, while she now sat in silence, no longer able to withstand the onslaught or grapple with her adversaries. Finally, Crysalle wearily stood up.

"Let's leave," she said slowly, defeated, worn out from the ordeal. "I think that's enough." So everybody left.

*   *   *   *   *

When Cousin Colenna called Crysalle the following Sunday, she got no answer. Wondering what might have happened, she went on over to the apartment and contacted the concierge.

"Oh, Miss Baltimore? She died two days ago, right there in her apartment. It was frightfully sad. Overdose of aspirin apparently. There was an empty bottle by her bed that had held 500 tablets, but it was empty."

"No, not Crysalle! She would never do anything like that."

THE END

Short Stories at Last

Oh, I Don't Either

Tennessee is in the middle of the Bible Belt; there is no doubt about that. A lot of people go to church in Nashville and Murfreesboro and Knoxville and such places, and many of them are rather religious. Martin Manning didn't know just how religious people can be until he moved to Knoxville a few years ago, to teach at the University of Tennessee branch campus there. But he soon learned that not everybody who goes to church has to be a religious devout, in the strict sense of being a "Believer." Some people who are not really believers can still be religious, that is, have religious feelings about the existence of a god, or some powerful creative force out there, or spirits in natural settings like woods and streams, or even powers behind the finer human emotions like love and caring and sympathy and kindness and peacefulness.

I suppose Martin might have been considered religious in a broad sense, but not in any specific sense. He could accept the idea of there being some sort of a creator or creative force behind the things he saw in nature, and even in the remarkable world of science, but he did not accept much of the material in the Bible that smacks of the supernatural or magical. Maybe there are other religious people, like Bishop John Spong, who don't believe that Jesus actually walked on water, if it was more than two inches deep. Or that anybody, even a god, could turn water into wine without making it into grapes first, or make blind people see by a touch of the hand, unless it was to lift a

199

turban that had slipped down over the fellow's eyes. Some of these things must have been symbolic, whatever that means. I guess it means not true, made up, or artificial and phony, like pretend.

If he thought about it, Martin Manning would have told you that religion is a fantastically elaborate structure, sometimes even quite beautiful, manufactured by the creative human mind, or rather thousands of minds, who originally felt a need for some reason for things they were ignorant about and could not understand or explain, as well as the need for something to give them hope and purpose in this apparently hopeless and purposeless life.

But Martin really felt the vast variety one finds in nature -- in botany and zoology, not to mention physical sciences and mathematics -- to be so vast and varied that it can soak up any amount of study and interest that anyone in his lifetime could possibly devote to it. Martin thought people should be satisfied with the remarkable and inexplicable things that they can see and feel and touch, without having to imagine the invisible and intangible. He saw no need for them to create in their minds elaborate structures that have no reality outside of their imagination and their faith. Martin once heard an Atheist's definition of faith. "Faith is believing what you know ain't so."[1] Martin thought that was pretty clever, but was wise enough to realize that a lot of people wouldn't like it, especially religious people. Some religious people even think you are somehow a better

_____

[1] Attributed to Prof. Robert V. (Bill) Daniels, University of Vermont (1926-2010)

person if you can believe something without seeing it than if you *can* see it. Try asking them what they think God gave us eyes and ears for . . . no, don't do that, that wouldn't be nice and they wouldn't like it.

But Martin would admit that religion has brought much beauty into the world, as well as much horror. How many wars and persecutions have been conducted in the name of God? Hitler's soldiers as well as those of his predecessor Karl Wilhelm II had the words "*Gott mit uns*" engraved on their belt-buckles. In the United States we even entrust our money to God, although the Bible tells us to eschew money and wealth. Read the words on a dollar bill or a coin some day. Trust in spiritual things is not enough. But religion has given us extravagantly beautiful architecture in churches and cathedrals. Religion has inspired the masterpieces of countless artists from Leonardo da Vinci and Michelangelo to Velasquez and El Greco. Music like Mozart's Requiem and Wagner's Parsifal could not have existed or would have been quite different had their composers no religion in their hearts.

In the normal course of events, after Martin settled in to his new job at the University in Nashville, and bought a little house in the suburbs, he did meet someone he found attractive. A woman, she was. The school librarian, about his own age. Sharon liked to read, the best-sellers anyway, and of course had a good supply of them. She was a quiet person, very pretty and only slightly overweight; she seemed to be very self contained and non-threatening. It was easy for Martin to meet her -- he often used the library in the normal course of events. In short, she was available, and he started dating her. He was delighted that she

201

enjoyed hearing his views on a multitude of subjects, sports and philosophy, and even politics. She had ideas and opinions that matched his closely and seemed almost invariably to dovetail nicely. Their friendship grew as they steadily got to know each other better, and gradually were getting closer to some serious romantic business. Martin knew she liked him, maybe even loved him; they were so much alike in their views of everything.

Almost everything.

Sharon was religious, and she went to church religiously, almost every Sunday. Roman Catholic, she was, although the Catholics are not so strong in that area of Tennessee as are many of the various fundamentalist Protestant sects. Martin avoided discussing religion with her; he didn't want religious differences to come between them. When he was a child, his family avoided religion as a subject for proper dinner table conversation, and rightly so, along with sex and politics. But, for him, there was another reason to avoid it. You see, Martin was an Atheist, in case I hadn't told you. He knew he was an Atheist because he didn't believe all that supernatural stuff you read in the Bible and hear in church. He did go to church now and then, but it was to be sociable with family and friends or to hear Haendel's "Messiah" or Dubois's "Seven Last Words" and other pieces of beautiful music that he loved. It bothered him that he liked the trappings of religion -- many of its outward and visible signs -- pictures of the beautiful Gothic cathedrals in Milan and Cologne and Orleans, the masterful paintings of Murillo and Rembrandt and Leonardo, the church music of Bach and Händel and even Mendelssohn, which he sometimes heard on the organ of the church right in town, not to mention the beautiful stained glass windows and statuary found in many churches. It bothered him to like these superficial things about religion without being able to accept the substance of religion itself.

When Martin was not around, Sharon would sometimes talk about her passionate beliefs, but she didn't want to upset Martin, and in his presence she generally limited her religious observations to the visible aspects that he had found attractive. In short, she agreed with him every chance she got. She wanted him to like her and accept her, and he did just that. He loved her, and accepted her, and was delighted that she always seemed to agree with his suggestions, points of view, philosophy, etc.

But Martin was uncomfortable with feeling his views of religion were superficial, touching only the tangible and visible beauty of religious adornments, while hers were profound, stemming from deep within the beauty of the heart. He began almost to feel that he was deceiving her, his dear one, who shared all his other feelings and ideas that he could think of.

Finally, one day he decides he can no longer be a hypocrite about religion, even if openness and honesty may cost him his dear love. He feels he must clear the air and bite the bullet and lay the cards on the table and face the music and let it all out and tell it like it is. He knows she is not going to like it, and knows it may be the end of the relationship, but he cannot bring himself to pretend he believes all that stuff when he doesn't. He doesn't believe in miracles any more than Thomas Jefferson did -- about the virgin birth, and Jesus rising from the dead, and making wine out of water, and making the blind see, and walking

203

on the water, and all that hooey and make-believe. The idea of life after death was certainly appealing, and is a soothing thought to carry in your head, especially when you are getting old and beginning to realize that sometime you really are going to die. You can smile there as you imagine yourself singing and dancing eternally among the angels, rejoining your old friends -- the good, devout ones anyway, who made it -- seeing your grandparents again, and getting to know your other ancestors from even further back. If you were a Muslim, perhaps you would be surrounded by everlastingly young nubile virgins bending over backwards for you, at your peck and call. No wonder there are so many suicide bombers in those countries over there, people eager to taste the enjoyment of the glorious Afterlife. No end of pleasure. Eternal.

So one evening when they have had supper and are sitting on the porch finishing off the wine, he lets it all out. He hates to hurt dear Sharon, but he can no longer live this overwhelming, oppressive lie. He tells Sharon that he can't take the Bible literally and that he doesn't believe all that stuff. "Never really did."

"Oh, Darling, neither do I. Never really did. I thought you knew."

THE END

The Candidate

I was never very involved in politics, especially in my younger days. Oh, we used to have discussions about everything when we were in college, but mostly in general terms rather than specifics. We discussed Communism and Racism, and Karl Marx and Franklin Roosevelt and Adolf Hitler. There were those who said every question or argument has two sides; however, in the Debating Society, the purpose was not to learn which side of a question was the correct or true side, but to see how well one could argue from either point of view. You should be neutral before being given one side to support and defend.

I did not always agree with this approach -- this theory. I felt, and contended, that there is a distinction between being neutral and being objective. One good example was Churchill and Hitler during World War II. I could try to be objective as I looked at the two sides and studied what they stood for, but I could not be neutral about it. It would not be a good subject for a debating society in which positions were assigned arbitrarily, or randomly. Better to debate about who enjoys romance more, men or women, or whether Baptists or Episcopalians have a better chance of getting into Heaven. Questions without much substance but with plenty of room for the expression of opinions and emotions, and of course eloquent elocution.

One of my friends, Preston Farmington, had a bright idea to use in discussing whether something might happen or not happen. It all started one evening when he said, hyperbolically, "I'd give a thousand dollars if we could beat Yale in football next Saturday."

"Really?" I said. "Is it really worth that much to you?"

"Well, maybe not a thousand dollars, but a lot anyway."

"How much, then?" I continued, pursuing the matter.

"What do you mean?"

"I mean, how much would it *really* be worth to you for us to be sure of beating Yale? If it's worth fifty dollars, go bet $50.00 on *Yale* to win. If we win, as you wanted, you have gotten your money's worth. If Yale wins, you have fifty dollars to take to Benny Haven's and drown your sorrows and buy drinks for everybody."

"Great idea."

* * * * *

I later learned that this practice is not so uncommon as you might think. Although I'm sure it's illegal, sometimes the owners of race horses bet on other horses to win over their own, figuring a win -- win situation, like hedging your investment in oil stocks. You bet gas prices will drop, by buying a "put" option. If values go up you are fine because your stocks are now worth more. If prices and values go down, your losses are mitigated or compensated for by the sudden increase in value of your put option. That is called hedging your bets.

I'm out of school now, and grown up, living in the middle of the USA. It's interesting that to most people the middle of the USA depends on their point of view. If you are from Memphis you may see Denver as the middle of the United States. If you are from Boston the middle of the US may be somewhere near Albany or perhaps Pittsburgh. Possibly Cincinnati. Everything beyond that is the West or the Far West.

Anyway, at some of our local elections, for City Council Members, for Mayor, for the County Commissioner of Education, and even for Governor, we do not always elect the best candidate for the position. I have sometimes thought back to my old friend Preston's idea of betting against your own wishes for something you wanted.

The present governor of our great state is a jerk, if I do say so myself. But, would you believe, I did bet on him to win. Oh yes I did. And I won $1,000, enough to drown my sorrows in Panama City for a weekend drinking and buying drinks for strangers with profligate abandon. Well, I would have been equally happy to lose that $1,000 to keep the jerk out of the Governorship and see my favorite get in.

It's a shame, isn't it, when our only choice often comes down to simply having to vote against someone or something we don't like. There may be no one, or nothing to vote *for,* that we particularly do like. We vote for the lesser of two evils, or sometimes the least of three or four evils. That's what I was thinking of at the last election. Yes, people vote for what they see as the lesser of the evils. They are not voting for something they like, but voting against something they don't like and don't want. It's like a litotes in grammar. I had done it myself, and then I started doing some more thinking about it.

If there is a really good, honest, forward-looking candidate in one of the elections -- the election for the governorship for instance -- he hasn't got much of a chance. The network of good old boys, and insiders, and established cliques and back-room operations, will see to that. The ones in power enjoy opportunities for a little corruption that keep them in power: payoffs, influence-peddling, powerful lobbyists, nepotism . . .

If a new face runs against the entrenched establishment, the odds are stacked against him. The propaganda machine, the press, and public opinion, are so dominated by forces in power in our state that he hasn't got a chance. The new face is painted as the greater of evils, and he will usually lose.

*   *   *   *   *

So, along with any influential friends I might have had back then, I decided to do something about it. The political party in power then was the Nationalists, and we, the Loyalists, wanted them out of the Governor's Mansion at any cost. The election was ten months away. I discussed my idea with my friends. We developed a plan.

We would focus on the primary gubernatorial election. The primary is sometimes more important that the final. There were already six terrible Nationalist candidates who had announced their intention to seek their party's nomination. One of them was so unqualified and such a scoundrel that almost everyone I knew said he didn't have a chance of a snowball in Laredo of winning the Nationalist nomination, let alone the election. The fellow's name was Roscoe Tolman. Now this Roscoe was quite well known locally. He knew a lot of people and he had done business throughout the state. He had somehow made a fortune overtly importing onyx ashtrays and Pancho Villa T-shirts from Mexico. He had won local fame by advocating the easing of laws controlling the importation of certain other substances as well. Further sources of his significant wealth were widely suspected but always well protected. Part of his fame or notoriety came as a result of the five years he spent in prison having been convicted of importing and selling -- in other words trafficking in -- "substances" that were illegal. Upon his release from prison, Roscoe Tolman soon proved to himself and to his friends how little the local townsfolk knew about, or cared about, the background or real nature of their political leaders. He ran for, and easily won, an empty seat on his city council that no one else seemed interested in. Two years later he got himself elected mayor. No one seemed to want to take on the responsibilities of these thankless jobs with their pitifully small remuneration. But Roscoe recognized their potential. A little money invested under the table into the right hands could bring a healthy financial return. There would be repair contracts for the city streets and sidewalks, maintenance of the city water system, storm sewers, shopping plaza building permits, garbage and trash collection. Opportunities abounded on every hand, some of them perfectly legal.

Anyone who looked beneath the surface into the life and activities of this fellow would realize that if the truth were known about this blackguard, this scoundrel, this social parasite, he would not stand a chance in an election for Dog Catcher if he were the only candidate.

That's how Roscoe Tolman fitted into our plan -- the idea I spoke about a while ago of intentionally betting on a loser. We would bet on Roscoe.

It was like the way the Americans were taught to hate the Japanese during World War II, a hatred that lingered on for many years in spite of the close post-war economic ties between the two countries. Americans were told repeatedly by radio announcements, billboards, grocery store placards, newspaper articles and pictures featuring Hitler and Tojo, "This Is Your Enemy." Ubiquitous jingles and bumper stickers were used to help sell patriotic Defense Bonds and War Bonds./1

Without revealing our true political orientation, of course, in January or February last year we started promoting the idea of Tolman for the Nationalist nominee as Candidate for Governor. We knew he was so bad he couldn't possibly win in the November election, and if he ran, our Loyalist Party candidate would be sure to win. We started by running articles in the local press with eloquent encomiums telling lies about what a wonderful governor Tolman would make. We knew we could easily refute them later, as well as other articles -- all lies – about how great his winning

---

/1 US Defense Bonds, later called War Bonds, were sold in denominations as low as $18.75 to be redeemed ten years later for $25.00, a poor financial investment considering inflation and interest rates. But patriotic.

chances would be if nominated by the Nationalists in the primary. Tolman got interested and got some of his old buddies together to set up a formal campaign structure, with a little office downtown on Main Street.

My friends and I supported the office with generous contributions -- anonymous, we thought best. Some of our own Loyalist members who were too young to have a voting record actually worked with Tolman's Campaign Committee, designing and distributing campaign slogans and literature, making phone calls, the whole bit. We had to do whatever it took to get Roscoe nominated as the Nationalist candidate for governor -- as he was sure to lose the election. All the polls said so.

And we did it! When the NSEC (Nationalist State Election Committee) met over the July 4 weekend, they nominated Roscoe Tolman to be their candidate for governor on the third ballot. We had done it!

Now all we had to do was stop telling lies about how great Tolman was, and tell the truth about what a scoundrel and crook he was. We had four months to do that. It would be easy and fun.

We set up a Loyalist campaign office and organized a Stop-Tolman movement. Our own Loyalist candidate, Christopher Alexander, was a good man, steady and thoughtful, who had served with distinction for ten years in our State Legislature, four years as a representative and six years as senator. He was known for his ability to bring opposing views together in compromise, for his concern for the well-being of the workers and common people, and for

211

his advocacy of sound fiscal management. He would make a good governor, what we needed. Although Alexander was quiet and effective in his way, and had never gained widespread publicity through the media, he nevertheless had very few enemies. It seemed that the masses of the public either liked him, tolerated him, or had never heard of him. Well, we would have to move the thinking public up that ladder a notch or two. They would be hearing more about him.

We founded our campaign on the phrase, "If The Truth Be Known." We purported to have the goal of positively supporting our candidate, Christopher Alexander, and we did support him, spreading the truth about his clean life, his devoted service to the State over the years, and his two children currently enrolled in state public schools.

But our real effort was to paint and spread scandalous truth about the shady and often illegal wheeling and dealing of that rascal, Roscoe Tolman. "Roscoe the Rascal" was one of the catchy labels we spread about. We told the awful truth about him, only slightly embellished on occasion for hyperbolic effect. We went back through the same channels we had used to build up Roscoe's candidacy for his nomination in the first place, this time tearing him down with the truth. We got articles into the local press, post office flyers, radio and TV announcements, and community debates -- all the things we had used before, the other way around.

We were more successful than we had ever imagined possible. The polls in September already showed the public favoring Alexander over Tolman 51 to 49. By mid-

October the polls made it 54 to 46, a healthy margin. And by the first of November Alexander was leading by the unheard-of landslide 61 to 39. We had done it!

That was when the second part of my idea kicked in. I knew that several times in American history a candidate had won the presidency with fewer than half the votes cast. Lincoln did it in 1860 with only 39.8% of the votes. Hayes won with 48% of the vote to Tilden's 52%. George Bush won with fewer votes than his opponent, Al Gore, and it seems that Trump may have done it too. I don't know if the same thing has ever happened in a gubernatorial election, but I suddenly shuddered at the thought of that possibility in our own state.

No, not a chance. Even though the voting system tends to favor the Nationalist candidate, Roscoe Tolman wouldn't have a chance. The polls were overwhelmingly in favor of Alexander. As the polls continued to move our way, the odds against Tolman shot up through the roof. Las Vegas had been quoting 2 to 1. Then 6 to 1. Then a high of 10 to 1. But still we didn't want to take any unnecessary chances. We continued to harp on Tolman's shortcomings, his previous record, his skulduggery, his unfitness, right up until Election Day. By then the odds against Tolman were almost 20 to 1. Unheard of.

But I did one other thing well. I remembered the advice of my old school friend Preston Farmington, in cases like this. Bet on the side you don't want. It's like hedging your bet. So I bet $1,000 on Tolman on the nose to win, with odds of 16 to 1. It was certainly worth that much to me to get Alexander into the governorship. It was my contribution to my state; my patriotic contribution to what was best for all our people. Alexander had to make it. It was well worth any old thousand dollars. With odds like that I stood to win $15,000 if Tolman won, less the bookie's commission of a few hundred, but it of course also meant that winning was very unlikely.

*   *   *   *   *

All that was a month ago. Now it is mid-December, and I am with my wife on a week-long Caribbean Viking cruise. I have just started to sober up slightly, and am trying to decide whether I like Margaritas or Rum Collinses the best. Tolman defied the polsters and, in spite of all our work, won the election by a razor-thin margin, only 400 votes, or less than half of one percent.

Then I heard on TV in the ship's lounge last night that the State Supreme Court has ordered a recount of the votes because of suspected fraud in half-a-dozen precincts. The news analysts say it appears the election results will be overturned.

Hooray!

So now it looks as though I went and got drunk for nothing. Hic. I had my cake -- I mean my margaritas -- and drank them too, when it wasn't even necessary.

Fantastic! Whoever would have thought . . .

THE END

Queen Bee

Tides rise and fall, and tides ebb and flow, one way then the other. Sometimes people do too, maybe most of the time. We expect people to be stable and consistent, but they're not – and we're not. We all have our vagaries and vicissitudes, our ups and downs. But we also change over time, some of us.

Beatrice was born in rural Alabama in 1946 on land that had been part of a prosperous cotton plantation in the old days. Cotton was rarely grown there anymore as it is such a labor-intensive industry. There was more land in that part of the county than there were farmers to farm it, or pickers to pick it, and some of the land simply lay fallow. But the soil was reasonably good, and the locals and their families were able to subsist by growing vegetables and tobacco in small plots of land that did not require much work.

As a child, Beatrice liked to go to school because the children who went to school didn't have to work so much around the farm. She also liked getting away from her two older brothers, who were always trying to boss her around and make her realize that they were better than she was. At home things were never equal and fair, as she thought they should have been. But at school she could begin to feel a sense of self-importance and in time let her natural leadership abilities grow and flourish. She rapidly gained stature in the eyes of her classmates, and by the time she was in middle school she began to realize that she was able

215

to start bossing *them* around. She liked the feeling of power and influence over others. In high school she was always the leader for her group when they were assigned "cooperative projects," and she always won any arguments about what games they were going to play at recess, or how the athletic events should be scheduled.

Academically she was an average student, but there was something about History that particularly aroused her curiosity and her interest. That was when she learned that Black folks, who were called Negroes or colored people back then, had come from distant lands on a far continent called Africa, starting many generations ago. She did not know it at the time, but this interest in Black heritage was to be an important influence on her life in years to come.

Her full name was Beatrice Hyacinth Beejandry. When she was a child in Alabama her family called her Bee, and that was all right with her. The name stuck in high school. The students at Bee's high school were mostly Black or colored;   that was in the early sixties before President Johnson tried to bring equality and integration into the public schools. When Bee was nineteen, she graduated from high school, one of few in her family to get a high-school diploma. One of her brothers and many of her cousins dropped out of school as young teenagers and just stayed around the farms or worked at odd jobs when they felt like it or had to. The farm held no attraction for Bee.

Shortly after her graduation she married a professional gambler, Kalumba Washington, who was good at his profession and made, or garnered, quite a bit of money at it. Kalumba didn't like his name very much, which may be understandable, so he told his friends to call him Kal. Bee liked not having to worry about money.

Bee loved her husband, Kal, but liked her own name and saw no need to take his name on top of hers. They were a happy couple and, although they never had any children, they liked people, Bee especially. Bee continued to be active in her church, and she baby-sat and helped care for her nieces and nephews, but her main interest and activity in the 1960's and 70's rested in the opportunities for showing her racial solidarity by participating in marches and demonstrations for equality. Paradoxical though it was, as Bee continued her energetic work for various tendentious groups, such as the NAACP, the NUL, and the Rainbow Push Coalition, that were devoted to the goal of spreading racial equality, her natural management talents and executive abilities stood her in good stead, and she rapidly rose in position and importance in these organizations. The inchoate leadership ability that she had felt budding in her school days now flourished and blossomed fully.

Even though by then a number of years had passed, Bee still remembered hearing in school that there was royal blood in the veins of some American slaves and their descendants. Bee never forgot these stories. They had intrigued her, and she felt -- she *knew* -- she must have royal blood in her own veins. What else could explain her preeminence and her superiority over her classmates and the others in her church? Where else did she get her dominant leadership qualities? Certainly not from her parents and grandparents; they were simple farmers and sharecroppers.

Having decided she had royal blood, she told Kalumba, her husband, that she wanted confirmation of what she already knew. Kalumba wisely made no objection; he was not in the habit of opposing any of his wife's desires or decisions.

Accordingly, with her husband's money, Bee engaged a genealogical research firm to trace her African origins. The researcher was glad to oblige. Like all such researchers, he was an expert in finding notable, or rich and famous, ancestors, among any people in any nation on any continent. He had conveniently found that many Americans, white as well as Black, had descended from kings and queens, even if they themselves had simply come to the New World to escape from Royal tyranny or to strengthen the American labor force. In 99.44 per cent of such cases, the best researchers gave their clients their money's worth and came up with precisely the ancestors their clients were hoping to find.

However, as any good African researcher knows, the number of African Americans who would have been kings or queens had their ancestors remained in Africa was considerably exaggerated. The researchers knew that over the centuries, and long before the time of Columbus, warring tribes of African natives used to capture young men and women of the opposing camp and sell them as slaves, as a means of earning money. For many tribes it was the major source of hard currency and foreign exchange. Of course it worked two ways: you capture mine and sell them, and I will capture an equal or greater number of yours and sell *them*. So all in all, it balanced out about even.

Some of the tribes had unofficial agreements with each other as to the acceptable level of slaves that were suitable for capture, sort of like a cod-fish quota. However, if the member of the family of a tribal leader, or a person of a royal family, were captured, he brought a much higher price as ransom material than he would have brought being sold as a slave -- typically three or four times as much. It just did not pay to sell royalty into slavery, and the fact is that few members of African royalty were ever exported as slaves to the United States, or to Brazil, or to any other country for that matter. This is not to say that many African Americans did not carry royal blood in their veins. Almost all had a few drops, for in Africa the extent of romantic affairs and illicit carryings-on in previous centuries transcended the formal stigmas of class strata and social boundaries just as it did in England and other supposedly civilized countries throughout the ages. It has been estimated that over sixty per cent of the people living in England in 1970 carried at least a drop of blood from William the Conqueror. (After 1970 the percentage dropped significantly with the massive influx of immigrants from the Middle East and North Africa, where William had never been.)

When Bee received confirmation of her royal African blood, she suddenly changed. She no longer marched for equality. She had proof that she was better than her neighbors and the other parishioners of her church. She began to take ever more forceful positions in handling social affairs and in dealing with her church vestry and indeed the pastor himself. She seized more power than ever in her favorite organizations that were working for racial equality. Her royal blood went to her head. She started bossing people around on every hand, and not just black African Americans, but also colored people, mulattoes, mestizos, half-breeds, and even uppity whites and high yellows. She claimed authority through her lineage. Among her friends and family and acquaintances her word was Law. She ruled the roost by Divine Right.

Her fame spread. The size of her church congregation doubled in less than three years, as visitors came to see, liked what they saw, were intrigued, and stayed. People in the United States, and not just white people, are fascinated by Royal Families of the Old World. Three times as many biographies of Edward VIII, and stories about Diana, have been bought and read in the United States as in the entire United Kingdom. African Americans are fascinated by the image of Black African kings and queens, and to have a queen right here in our midst in Alabama became a major attraction.

As Bee became ever more popular, people started calling her the "Queen Bee," and she loved it; the name seemed to have a certain buzz to it that she found particularly *à propos* and copacetic.

As she increased her authority and began to throw her weight around, she gained a few pounds -- quite a few. Never having been a wispy thing, she gradually went from 138 to 183 pounds over the next few years, and kept on going after that. Anyway, has anyone ever seen a woman who was Deaconess of the African Church of the True Believers, or Director of the Holy Southern Gospel Singers, who was not stout, or portly, or maybe even somewhat obese? Her physique gave her greater confidence and charisma along with increased strength of will and more awesome appearance. She was every inch the Queen.

220

Then, as the membership of the little church continued to expand, it acquired a new assistant pastor, to help handle the growing congregation. His name was Lumumba Lincoln. He was three or four years younger than Bee, and the Queen didn't expect him to give her any problems.

Now this young Rev. Lincoln had been a racial activist and had met Bee some years before in marches and peaceful banner-waving demonstrations. He was an avid advocate of equal rights in principle, although he did not always push the bus-riding undertaking as energetically as did Bee and others. As a matter of fact, when Linc was a lad, he rather liked riding in the back of the school bus, for there he could sit next to his girlfriend and they could hold hands and fool around where nobody could see them, or at least the driver couldn't see them. But he was dismayed and disappointed in Bee when she started getting her uppity ideas about her royal heritage and no longer acted as the equal of other people, because indeed, she knew she wasn't.

Lumumba extolled Abraham Lincoln and preached that he was the greatest advocate of equality we have ever had, accusing Bee of deviating from Lincoln's strait and narrow path. So he argued with her, and their friendship expired. That's when he burst forth espousing a great idea of Abraham Lincoln's, and told her she should go back to Africa if she could not accept equality here in the good ole USA.

You see, Lumumba Lincoln was deeply devoted to following in the footsteps of his namesake, Abraham, and opposed the idea of superiority -- royal superiority, or racial superiority, or any other kind of superiority. He realized,

221

and preached, that Blacks and whites are equal. However, he also acknowledged the sad truth that Blacks among themselves are not all equal, although of course they should be. For this he cited Bee as living proof. He might have added that not all whites are equal either, but that was not his concern. As he expressed these views, he generated a major confrontation with the Queen Bee as well as her supporters and admirers.

The Reverend Lincoln didn't know what kind of a hornets nest he was getting into through his vociferous opposition to Bee. The Queen wasn't going to let this little upstart, pastor or not, cast aspersions upon her, or push her around and tell *her* what to do. She decided he would have to go.

After eighteen months of severe litigation, during which the Rev. Lincoln engaged the best legal defense his limited funds could afford, the forces loyal to the Queen removed him from his position as Assistant Rector in the African Protestant Church of the South (APCS), and he had to seek employment elsewhere.

In his parting bitter diatribe directed at the Queen Bee, as quoted in the *Savannah Evening News* and the *Atlanta Constitution*, he bellowed, "Why don't you go back to Africa, like Abraham Lincoln wanted, 160 years ago? And take all your royalty views and prejudices with you. We don't need royalty in our democracy in the United States of America! We have laws here and everybody is equal!"

The words of the Reverend Lumumba Lincoln were picked up by all the local newspapers and a number of national papers as well, from the *Boston Globe* to the *Los*

222

Angeles Times. However, his efforts were counter productive. All he did was to give a great deal of additional publicity to the Queen Bee and her entourage: the power and the influence of her little empire tripled in size and importance over the next two years, and is still growing. She did go back to Africa once, but only for a visit. Strangely, she was not very well received in Liberia or even Ghana, where some rude people refused to recognize her claim to royalty and fame and told her, to her face, to "go back home to wherever she came from."

Several years later, after Lumumba had done more reading up on the life of his beloved namesake, he was shocked, and also quite perturbed, to learn that Abraham Lincoln did not espouse racial equality as much as he had thought. In fact, Lincoln even said he was glad he was white, since the white race was the superior one, or words to that effect./1

But by then it was too late for the Rev. Lumumba Lincoln to change his mind or apologize and take back what he had said to poor Bee. She had already died -- diabetes and heart failure. She was 47 years old. Now he would have to wait a while before he could see her again. In the meantime he might at least think about changing his name.

THE END

/1 On September 18, 1858, in the famous Lincoln Douglas Debates, Lincoln declared that, when two races come together: *"There must be the position of the superior and the inferior; and I, as much as any other man, am in favor of the superior position being assigned to the white man."*

Forgiveness

"Be swift to love;
make haste to be kind."
-- Henri Fédéric Amiel

What a relief! Sammy had been carrying a weighty burden for three decades, and now the load was off and he was free to let his spirits return and his heart and soul become human -- and humane -- once again.

Sammy Samuelson had been suffering from a vindictive grudge all those years, and from the inanition of its deleterious effect upon his spirit, his soul, and even his physical health. It took him a long time to realize it, but to continuously carry hate in your heart is to carry a corrosive acid that inexorably despoils and erodes the core of your being, destroying your humanity and even your health in the process. Sammy had borne that hate for almost thirty years, hating and loathing one particular object -- one particular thing -- one particular human being -- his ex-wife, Sally, in particular. Throughout those years, he was living on his hate for her, treasuring it, savoring it, enjoying the thought of every nasty thing she had done to him, everything that added to his hatred and justified his bitterness toward that wretched creature, his wife. His ex-wife, that is. Years of carrying a millstone around his neck, damaging no one but himself.

He lost weight. He lost his job. He was unable to think and concentrate on what he was doing or was supposed to do. But that didn't matter. He was reveling in his hatred for her. He was an addict and hate was his drug -- his cocaine. He couldn't live without it. He sucked it up. It sucked him up. Hate was his life blood and his blood-sucker at the same time.

Sammy had not been the one to seek the divorce, but, after it became final, he thought he would make the best of it. He tried to tell himself that in spite of the devastating financial cost of the lawyers and the court case, the outcome is not so bad after all. Now, being single, with complete freedom, he would make new friends, have new mistresses, go places and do things that were unknown to him under his former married life. But that was just talk, and it didn't work out. Sally had been everything to him. His love for her was complete, his happiness over the years with her had been without equal -- *nonpareil.* So his new freedom brought no joy. His bitterness and hatred were too powerful; they transcended his entire being, penetrated to the core. He could not turn it on and off. It was there, the one constant in his life, dominating him completely, eating into his heart and soul, isolating him from any human relationships or humane thoughts. He became a recluse, almost a hermit. Few faithful family members would even talk to him; or he to them.

* * * * *

The occasion of Sammy's first meeting with Sally was one you would have been more likely to find in a Danielle Steele romantic novel than anywhere in real life. It happened directly under God's watchful eye in the beautiful Anglican Church of "Saint Paul's within the Walls" in beautiful Rome, where Sammy was working at the American Embassy, in the heart of beautiful Italy, on a beautiful Sunday morning in early spring. Their beautiful, unforgettable, storybook meeting lasted only one day -- only one afternoon of sightseeing -- for, promptly the next morning, Sally and her chaperon -- her mother -- were scheduled to be off again with their tour group to quickly visit four more countries before flying back home to Sydney. To be polite and show his admiration for this pretty young Australian maiden, quick-thinking Sammy asked her for her home address, which he meretriciously wrote down in his little black notebook, never really believing he would ever have the opportunity to use it. However, he was mistaken on that point.

* * * * *

Months passed.

Sally had forgotten about that day in Saint Paul's Church, when, over two years later, she suddenly received a letter from Saigon in an unknown handwriting. Some stranger named "Sammy" was telling her that he had met her in Rome and wanted to see her again. Sally's mother had to help remind Sally who this "Sammy" was. Apparently he had impressed the mother as much as the daughter, maybe more. Sammy was still in the Diplomatic Service, now working in Saigon and contemplating a little vacation trip to Australia. It was the mother who decided that proper social and diplomatic considerations behooved her and Sally to befriend this nice clean-cut young chap who was in

Vietnam helping Australia's good old faithful ally, the United States, to stem the spread of International Communism and impede its impending threat to the Australian Continent.

Upon his arrival Down Under, Sammy soon found himself being wined and dined at a lovely little welcoming reception given by Sally and her mother -- albeit mostly the mother. Sally was delighted and impressed by the graceful manner in which Sammy was able to fit in and socialize with all these unknown people -- her friends and extended family. All had a jolly good time. The ball had started rolling. Sammy saw Sally every moment he could for the next several days, and was soon completely heels over head in love. Before the end of the fortnight he asked her to marry him, just as her mother had expected.

Sammy had to interrupt his blossoming love affair and return to Vietnam to finish some work he was involved in, but after a few weeks he came back, and they had a lovely wedding at Sally's favorite church, St Mark's, right there in Sydney's Eastern Suburbs. He thereupon promptly took his bride on a honeymoon trip to Bangkok and then on to Beirut, Paris, and London, and finally the United States -- to Washington, DC, where he had a new assignment waiting for him and where he could show Sally the Washington Monument and the cherry trees.

Some of Sally's friends were dismayed to see her "run off" with this strange American in such a hurry. Why she married him, no one ever really knew. She wasn't even pregnant, but said little about the affair. Perhaps he did sweep her off her feet, and furthermore her mother thought he looked like "a good catch," even if he was a foreigner. Maybe at age 26 Sally was afraid of becoming an old maid, or maybe she just wanted to get out of her mother's house for a change. It is hard to know why women do things. But she did it. She married him, right there in her own beloved Episcopal church on Darling Point.

* * * * *

Sammy was in heavenly bliss. His happiness lasted quite a number of years, and Sally seemed happy too. They had a lovely daughter who filled any gaps in Sally's busy day. Sammy's position and connections enabled them to belong to a number of clubs and social groups that Sally enjoyed. It is understandable that Australians admire and appreciate social status and nice society, as well as money, given the humble origins of so many of them -- not all of them, of course, but a good many of them.

But unfortunately, after seventeen years of this, Sally decided she had had enough or wanted something more or different. She had tried to maintain a smiling face and an agreeable disposition throughout all these years, always dutifully accepting her husband's whims and preferences and seeming always to agree with his decisions regarding their politics, their finances, their dwelling places (they moved around a lot with his job), their choice of boats and automobiles, the selection of schools for their daughter. Besides all this, she had to put up with her husband's habit of looking at other women from time to time at social events and cocktail parties, and possibly in other recondite locations as well, who knows? She could never be sure that that was all he was doing -- just looking, and it became

229

a source of constant worry on her mind, almost an obsession. It wasn't that he took time away from their moments together; indeed, their intimate activities often seemed somewhat to exceed what she thought adequate for that sort of thing. But it is always comfortable and satisfying to have something big and important to worry about, so you don't have to worry about a lot of little things all the time. So Sally seemed glad to have the idea of Sammy's possible wayward activities to worry big about.

On one of their vacation trips he drove her to New England, where, among other things, she saw the house his grandfather had had built in 1913. It was a stately home, three storeys, six or seven bedrooms, the grandest house on the block, practically a mansion. "Sammy must have a lot of money besides his salary," was the thought that came to this Australian wife, as indeed it would have come to many practical, materialistic Australians. It gave Sally something else to worry about, as she thereafter realized that Sammy must be holding out on her financially, and she worried for the next ten years that he had more money than he acknowledged. "He must be salting it away somewhere but keeping me in the dark," she mused.

When the marriage began to get boring, Sally decided she must do something. She must find out a few things, especially about money: how much did Sammy really have? Sammy had always given Sally whatever money she needed, and more, but he thought it "wasn't nice" as a topic of conversation.. However, she knew that that was just his way of hiding it.

After Sammy retired from thirty years with the US Government, he supplemented his retirement pension by working from time to time as a substitute teacher in a Navy education program. Sally then did some pondering. She concluded that her husband was having a secret affair: she had no evidence beyond her woman's intuition, but that was enough. She had read stories about what men were like, and she *knew*. She also learned that the divorce laws in a neighboring state were more favorable to the woman, and without Sammy's knowing, as he was away at the time, she quietly claimed a new residence.

Even before she decided that Sammy was probably holding out on her financially, she had wisely been building up a tidy savings account of her own, unbeknownst to her husband. She increased it by several thousand dollars when she helped Sammy with the sale of their Ford Taunus station wagon when they had to leave Europe. Although almost brand new, the European model did not meet certain different US importation standards. She told him she had been able to get only one-third of the amount she actually did receive for the sale of the car. Easy money for her secret account, or "security cushion," as she herself viewed it. And Sammy, gullible and confiding as he was, believed her, without ever asking to see a copy of the bill of sale. For many years she would slightly exaggerate household expenses of all sorts, gradually adding to her secret savings. Just before the day she was to swing into action and have the sheriff serve her husband with divorce papers, she maxed out their credit card account, bringing several thousand dollars more into her own pocket. Sammy would learn of the seriousness of his wife's intentions when he discovered that his credit card would not work one rainy day when he needed to buy gas. Boy oh boy, wouldn't he just!

Some months earlier, Sammy had noticed an envelope on her desk with the return address of a law firm that apparently dealt in divorce cases. Quite surprised and astonished, Sammy asked her if it were possible she wanted a separation or was thinking of filing for a divorce. "Oh no," she said, laughing it off. "Why would I want a divorce? That's just a letter from an Australian friend of mine who happens to be working as a secretary there in the law office. She's a penny-pincher and sometimes uses company stationery to save money." It sounded like a typical Australian, thought Sammy, so he did not pursue the matter, nor look inside the envelope. He didn't think it was proper to intrude into another person's mail, even his wife's, although Sally never had such compunctions and was not reluctant to open and peek when her curiosity and an opportunity occasionally came together with mail addressed to her husband. Sally never mentioned divorce again . . . until one day . . .

A couple of weeks later, she said she would like to "talk about finances" with him. Fine, thought Sammy. He had been paying the rent and household bills as well as giving her $700 a month spending money to use when he was away teaching. (That was in 1984 when a dollar was worth four of today's dollars.) "Good that she is interested," he thought.

"Let's talk about it this afternoon, at five o'clock," she said. That sounded a little strange to Sammy; his wife was generally rather vague about time, but he didn't ponder the point.

232

Without Sammy's knowledge, so that it would be a surprise, she scheduled a visit from the friendly county sheriff to serve the papers late one afternoon when she knew Sammy wasn't teaching and would be relaxed and available after working all day on his boat. Furthermore, to make sure that he didn't run off at this critical moment and escape her plans for him, she hid the oars to his dinghy, knowing he could never sail away without the dinghy and its oars.

She had a tall cool highball with his favorite Irish whiskey ready for him at five o'clock as he came in after working out in the rain all afternoon, something nice she often liked to do for him in the good old days. When she had him comfortably seated, with a good strong drink in his hand, Sally slipped off to the kitchen to make a telephone call. At 5:10 another party arrived at the door, namely the County Sheriff, with an ominous manila envelope under his arm. "This is my husband, Samuel Samuelson," said Sally, gesturing toward the other man there in the room.

"Mr. Samuelson," said the sheriff, "I have something for you," as he shoved the envelope into his mid-section. The truth hit Sammy like a thunderbolt. So, that letter from the lawyer's office on her desk last month was not from a school friend of Sally's. She had planned the whole thing.

"But," he protested, dropping the papers without reading them, "she can't bring suit here; we are still residents of Texas. She signed residence papers there just three months ago."

"That's not my business," said the nice sheriff, insisting that it was his duty merely to deliver the papers.

Sammy shot a glance at Sally, as though to ask, "What the Hell is this?" as she was sidling back toward the kitchen, giving him simply her sweet little Mona Lisa smile backed by an air of satisfaction reminiscent of Little Jack Horner having just pulled a plum out of the Christmas pie.

Needless to say, Sammy was furious. "You want a divorce? What are you doing? Let's talk it over. We're not even separated, are we? You really want a divorce? Besides, we can go to a mediator. A mediator can save us a lot of money, whether we get a divorce or not. Why can't we talk about this? You never told me you were this unhappy. How long have you been wanting a divorce and planning this? Who put you up to it? Who have you been talking to?" Sammy's wrath was going over the top in his sudden fury and frustration. Sudden anger on top of his love for this dear sweet person that he cared so much for, who was such a part of his life, who *was* his life, who was now acting so strange.

"Let's let the lawyers work it out," she said demurely, without raising her voice.

Sammy stormed out of the house and back to his boat, furious, devastated, and completely confused.

* * * * *

The divorce went just about as Sally had planned. She had the most expensive lawyer she could find, and Sammy

234

had to get an expensive lawyer too. The lawyers demanded evidence of all Sammy's financial assets, apparently mentally constructing four piles: one for each of the litigants, and one for each of the lawyers. Sammy had to sell his real estate investments which he had been relying upon for his old age. Sally's lawyer had found and misrepresented a legal clause declaring that any assets acquired during a marriage became conjugal property, equally divisible, conveniently disregarding the exclusion if the purchase was made using pre-existing financial resources. (Sammy had inherited a small sum of money from his grandfather that was the basis of his real estate investments.) Sally got the house they lived in and a cash award that Sammy could meet only by selling off his other properties. Goodbye retirement income.

Sally refused to speak to Sammy after she had the papers served. "You will have to talk to my lawyer," was all she would say. Sally's lawyer was a woman, so Sammy thought he would be clever and fight fire with fire, so he also got a woman lawyer in a big law firm. Not such a smart idea, as it turned out. His lawyer had her own heart on the money clock, charging his account for every six minutes, every tenth of an hour that she spent "on the job," whether talking to Sammy on the phone, or opening his letters, or adding up the value of his assets, or dividing them into fourths. Being a woman herself, her underlying emotional sympathies were with the woman in any divorce process, but Sammy didn't realize that until it was all over and the smoke began to clear. They were now divorced, and Sally and her lawyer had been able to garner the equivalent of Sammy's entire salary from the thirteen years he was married to her while serving as an employee of the

US Government. That included the alimony he had to pay as well, plus the expense of two years private prep school for their daughter during the divorce process, to be followed by college costs which were also assigned to him.

Sammy felt financially and emotionally demolished. How unfair it all had been. How could Sally treat him this way, after all he had done for her and after he had loved her so? He had acquaintances whose wives got divorces with good reason, but left their naughty husbands without wanting anything but their freedom -- just wanting to get away. But not Sally. Sammy was not a naughty man. There had been only one other woman he had ever looked at with serious romantic thoughts, a woman Sally never knew about, although she had often falsely accused Sammy of having affairs with other women she had caught him talking to at cocktail parties at the Club, or looking at at the Marina or somewhere. But Sally wasn't going to let him off easy. She would get everything she could. That was the reason for the expensive lawyer, one of the best in the state. Sammy wondered how long she had been planning this, and in the subsequent weeks and months and years his inner fury and righteous indignation continued to seethe to the boiling point, dominating his thoughts and scorching his soul, gnawing at the remnants of the consuming love he had once held for her.

As the years went by, Sammy's deep love for Sally turned into deep hatred, bitter hatred, hatred that continued to grow and burn until it was a cancerous obsession, a devilish Dybbuk that took over his soul and was relentlessly corroding and eating out his heart and mind from within.

Sammy lost weight, while Sally, already comfortably overweight, gently continued to put on even more. Sammy's hair turned gray in a year. The few times he tried to play golf, his average score was between 110 and 120, whereas it used to be in the low nineties and high eighties. The poor man was unable to overcome or forget his hateful thoughts about this woman, and they festered in his mind and heart and in his golf stance. Oh, how he despised her! Loathed her. Detested her.. She was so unfair! Schemer!. That's the way it was and that's the way it remained for many years. Bitterness and venom were consuming Sammy's life. He couldn't even enjoy his freedom.

*   *   *   *   *

Sammy was never a particularly religious person, and now he rarely went to church at all. Sally had been the religious one in the family, and was the one who back then had seen to it that they went to church together fairly regularly. But one day, a Sunday, after all these years, Sammy wandered into church again on his own, and actually got interested in what the priest had to say. In his sermon the priest talked about love and forgiveness, citing appropriate quotations from the Scriptures. It seemed to Sammy as though his words were aimed directly at him. Interestingly enough, the priest did not rely upon any passages relating to supernatural powers or magical events, as so many priests and counselors do, and Sammy liked that. But his insightful ideas on love and forgiveness and what they can do to a person's life got Sammy thinking.

After church that day he went home and thought about it some more. His position in the universe began to clarify

237

for him. He had been out of it. Perhaps he should think of doing something to make himself human again. His current lifestyle was taking him to Hell. Was it possible that love or forgiveness could halt his descent and make a human being of him again? He knew he was a wreck, and what he heard in church that morning seemed focused right at him, to save him from the disastrous condition that hate had dragged him into. He started by deciding not to think about his ex-wife. If he did not think about her, maybe he could stop hating her or ultimately even forgive her.

So that's what he did; he put her out of his mind.

After several months he felt that he was getting a little better, just by not thinking of her. He sensed his hate for her beginning to abate. You cannot hate someone if you are not thinking of them. Then after a while, concentrating on the idea of love and caring for other people, his thoughts went on further, and, for the first time in years, he could once again think of his ex-wife without hating her and detesting her -- if he didn't think too hard.

Just because of the sermon that day, he began to undergo a remarkable change in his feelings, his health, and his entire well-being. He realized that as Christ loves us, we should love one another, even love and forgive in our hearts ex-wives who did not appreciate all we had done for them over the years. Sammy was soon able to forgive her in his heart and to think of her without despising her, especially if he limited his thoughts to the halcyon days of their early love. He began to regain his spiritual and emotional strength as well as his physical strength. His appetite returned. He regained half of the pounds he had lost. He

238

found new friends and restored relationships with old friends of years past. He was a new man, with joy in his heart once again and love in his soul -- love of the Lord Jesus and love of his neighbors and strangers, even Catholics and Black African-Americans and National-Socialists and Jews and Jehovah's Witnesses and even his ex-wife.

And now he was free, free of this insidious bond of hatred. Our Heavenly Father had taken pity on him and had spoken to him through his son Jesus Christ. This obsessive burden of vindictive spite and venom was being lifted from his shoulders and his spirit. Once again, after years of bitter disgruntlement and hatred, he saw beauty and light in the world. A new sunrise of love and forgiveness. He walked again with a youthful bounce to his step. He broke 100 on the golf course for the first time since the divorce, years ago. Yes, life could still be beautiful. Or rather, life could *again* be beautiful.

When Sammy had almost completely overcome his obsessive hatred, he began to consider calling Sally to tell her that he didn't hate her anymore. Perhaps she too had been suffering all these years, if she realized how much this man, whom she had once loved, now loathed and despised her. Perhaps he ought to tell her that he was sorry he had held such animosity in his heart for so long. Poor thing, she probably had been patiently waiting, anxiously hoping someday to hear the comfortable words of forgiveness coming from her ex. He had never told her that he hated and despised her, but but she probably knew -- probably had sensed it. Women have keen intuition, even if they are not always able to reason things out. Sammy was even thinking of sending her some flowers, because if she was still alive she might remember she had once been his wife.

With his heart now filled with a renewed spirit of compassion and grace, he decided he would do it; he would swallow his pride and open up his heart once again, his tight little heart that had been closed down in bitterness for so many years. He put an innocuous note in with her next monthly alimony check saying it might be nice to meet and have a chat. He said he would give her a call in a day or two.

So he did. He called her up. It would not be exaggerating to say that she was somewhat surprised, but Sally was not a woman given to revealing her emotions unnecessarily, and took his call as a matter of course. A free meal? she thought. "Why not?" she replied with the equanimity as of yore, not even particularly curious as to the purpose of the invitation after all these years. Sammy offered to pick her up at her apartment at eight o'clock next Thursday evening, but she said she would rather meet him somewhere, perhaps not wanting to show too much interest all of a sudden.

He would take her to dinner at an expensive restaurant. He would make a reservation at Stapleton's Skylight Dining Room, on the top of the Hyatt Hotel downtown. He would arrange with Frederika the Florist to have a grand bouquet of flowers sent ahead to the restaurant to adorn the table he was reserving with candlelight and wine. He would show Sally that he had no hard feelings and that his heart was filled with forgiveness and compassion, maybe even love. He began to feel a new joy like nothing he had

240

known in decades, with a warm and relaxing comfort sweeping over him, soothing him as it released all feelings of bitterness and loathing that had been stifling and stultifying his spirit and soul for so many months and years. It was as though he had been released from a prison, as though he had returned from the dying and the dead into a new life of sunshine and flowers and love and godliness. As he went into Stapleton's Skytop dining room at 8:25 that Thursday evening, he was happy as he had not been since the day of his marriage, so many years before.

Then something happened.

As he came into the restaurant he was delighted to see that they had prepared his table for two with a beautiful bouquet of roses and flowers in season next to the big picture window overlooking the city. She will like this, thought Sammy. But before he could speak to the hostess or a waiter, he was a little surprised to see Sally already there, sitting at a different table with another woman, a friend he did not know. "So," thought Sammy, "I guess she feels she needs moral support. All right, so what?"

Sally's back was turned and she did not see Sammy approach, but he was able to hear her laughing and saying, ". . . and I wish I could have seen his face when he was trying to buy gas and found out that I had taken $5,000 from his credit card account and maxed it out."

Sammy turned and quietly stumbled out of the restaurant. "Why should I spoil her evening's enjoyment?" he said to himself, as his mouth filled with blood from a hole he had bitten in his lower lip.

241

Sammy would have to rethink his recent spiritual renewal. Maybe he had carried it too far.

THE END

TNS Society

I am one of the lucky few who have ever been accepted and become members of the Triple Nine Society, TNS, a small group of intelligent people who meet periodically to enjoy good conversation, exchange of ideas, and simple social contact with one another. Not only that -- I am a woman, in a group where men outnumber women two to one, and where I have opportunities to show that women can think -- and talk -- as intelligently as men or anybody else. The TNS is so small that many people, perhaps most people, in the United States anyway, probably never heard of it.

Accordingly, I was surprised to see a strange TNS bumper sticker in the outback of Montana one sunny day last summer.

* * * * *

My name is Belle. Belle Fontaine. Belle is a truncated version of a long French name that I don't like, and I decided to strip it down for the benefit of my classmates as well as myself when I was in high school. That was a long time ago; I'm 38 now, hoping to reach 40 before I get too old.

I'm a design engineer working in Minneapolis for a little European company that makes flash hot-water heaters, the kind that heat the water just as you are using it, without the need for filling a big wasteful hot water tank. It is a somewhat unusual but interesting job.

One of my extra-curricular sources of mental stimulation comes from TNS, the Triple Nine Society, that my husband -- while he was still alive -- talked me into joining. It's a small organization, spread thinly throughout the civilized world. It holds periodic regional and annual gatherings in such far-flung places as Little Rock, San Diego, Orlando, Heidelberg, and Palma de Majorca.

When weather permits, I like to spend my vacations out of doors, and last summer, for a change, I decided to go camping on Montana's remote Northern Peninsula./1

One day, after enjoying a swim in the chilling refreshing waters of Flathead Lake, I was surprised to see a car parked near mine wearing a TNS bumper sticker such as I had never seen before. TNS people can be creative, and sometimes get ideas for new gadgets – things like buttons, coffee cups, and bumper stickers -- to put their labels and logos on.

I was rather surprised, for I didn't know any TNS members who were from Montana, or North Dakota either, for that matter. As I said, it's a small organization.

Just at that moment a nice-looking young man came up to the car, saw me inquisitively looking, and politely said, "Can I help you?"

/1 This is a fictional story.

"Oh," said I, "I see you are a member of TNS. I was looking at your bumper sticker," I added unnecessarily, for it was obvious what I was doing.

"Yep," he replied, apparently in all honesty. "I been a member going on fifteen years."

"Since you were very young then," I said, to keep the conversation going. The chap looked barely thirty years old.

"Yeah, I guess."

"I'm a member of TNS too. Belle. Belle Fontaine."

"Henry O'Hare, but everybody calls me Hank, for obvious reasons," he said with a smile, brushing back a lock from his forehead and sticking out his other hand.

"I don't think we've met," I said seriously, surprised to find a fellow TNS member out here that I had never even heard of. Well, I don't know everybody.

Henry laughed at that one, thinking I was trying to be cute, and replied, "Ha ha, no I don't think so. But now we have. So now, you want I should buy you a hot dog or a coke?"

Well, I thought, why not? If he's TNS he must be all right, in spite of his somewhat unusual accent. I have never met a TNS member I didn't like, and it seemed remarkable that I should meet this one out here in the sticks. Strange that he was alone perhaps, but then, I too was alone. Just as strange as he. "That might be quite nice," I demurely replied. "A cup of tea, perhaps."

So we went over to the fast-drink stand at the end of the parking lot. Hank -- he was Hank by then -- Hank got his hot dog and a coke; no beer allowed outdoors in Montana, he explained, and I settled for a can of Lipton's iced tea -- yuck. "We don't make hot tea in the summer," the kiosk girl helpfully added. We paid for our fare and took it to a bench under a shady sycamore tree, sat down, and looked at each other, both of us interested in our strange meeting like this.

Hank wasn't bad looking, had a nice smile, a good suntan, and a good physique. He looked more like an outdoors man than many of my other TNS friends and acquaintances did. "What do you <u>do</u>?" was the stock question we asked each other, as do all Americans everywhere.

I told him a bit about my work designing hot-water heaters, then looked at him and said, "Your turn."

"I've done, like, a lot of things," said Hank. "My first job outta high school was as an artist's model, but, you know, that was very inactive. Later, like when I was in California, I got some bit parts in the movies, boy-next-door types, you know, but that didn't go far. About then I took a course in Massage Therapy, and for the last few years I been, like, working in a massage place in Bismark. *'Tone Up Parlor'* it's called, right downtown on Custer Street. It pays good money, but, you know, I like to get out-of-doors when I can."

246

"My," I said, "but it does sound as though you have had -- and are having -- an interesting life." What I was mostly thinking was what a wide range of personality types one can find hidden in far corners of the TNS.

"What do you do when you're not designing magic water heaters?" he politely inquired.

"Lately I have started tutoring a few college aspirants for their entrance examinations, like the SAT."

"College aspirants?"

"Kids aspiring to get into college. Students preparing to take the SAT or ACT.

"Oh yes, the SAT," he said vaguely."

"I like tutoring, and I'm thinking of devoting myself to it full time. SAT and ACT, and maybe GRE and GMAT too. I find them all interesting, and not very difficult; you probably do too."

"I'm not sure. The SAT . . . that's a test, isn't it? And the ACT . . . is that another test, like, or what?" he asked, seemingly unsure of what I was talking about.

I was astonished. I could not imagine that any TNS member would not know what SAT and ACT were. But then, gems in the rough may turn up any place, and certainly not all TNS people are actively involved in education. Maybe I was proving it right there. Or maybe Hank had had an accident when he was younger, and fell

247

and hit his head while posing for the artist, so he is not so smart as he used to be. Or maybe he lost some of his memory because of all the noise from the cameras when he was in Hollywood making movies. You only have to show 999 evidence once to get into TNS; you don't have to keep proving it all your life.

That was when he changed the subject, and brought the focus back on me. "You know, it doesn't look like you've been getting out with any TNS groups for quite a while."

"Getting out?" I repeated questioningly, with my eyebrows slightly contracted. "I haven't been to any TNS gatherings at all yet this year, if that's what you mean."

"I mean getting out in the sun," and his eyes emphasized the point by roaming over his own well-tanned forearms and the sides of his sun-brown thighs. "I get out with my TNS friends all the time, you know, although this is the first time I have ever, like, been here at Flathead Lake."

By now I was having trouble making sense out of what Hank was talking about. "In fact," he said, "there is a camp on the other side of the lake, you know, that I was thinking of going to, but it seems that single men are not welcome, and my girl friend couldn't, like, get away and come up here with me this weekend. Maybe you would like to, you know, come with me. As my guest, of course. The name of the place is, SUNNY HAUNCHES NATURE CAMP, WHERE ANYTHING GOES, OR NOTHING."

My astonishment was overridden by a new view of this remarkable man. "You are the most amazing TNS person I have ever met."

248

"Amazing . . . ? What's amazing about me?" he said in typically modest TNS fashion. "All my friends in The Naturist Society enjoy upscale nudist camps like SUNNY HAUNCHES, and I'm sure you will too. They say the owners there bend over backwards to make sure everybody has a good time. Besides, you're rather pale. You could use some sun."

"The Naturist Society?" I stammered, as I choked on the last of my can of Lipton's tea.

"I'll have to think about it."

THE END

The Peace Commission

There has been a great deal of talk about the Civil War over the years. The Civil War was certainly the most important event -- if it can be called an event -- in the history of the United States.

Now, in the twentieth and twenty-first centuries, we think we know a lot about war, as we remember living through the bloody battles of Vietnam, Afghanistan, and Iraq, not to mention our incursions in Granada and Panama. Some of us who are older even remember living through World War II and Korea. And there are many more Americans who would be old enough, but don't remember these wars because they were killed and, as far as we know, can no longer remember anything. Yes, a lot of Americans have lost their lives in our wars. Many of them heroically gave their lives for their country, some of them had their lives rudely taken from them against their will, including many who fought in World War I, the Spanish-American War, the Black Hawk Indian War and the Sioux War, the Mexican War, the Seminole Indian War, the War of 1812, and of course the Revolutionary War, perhaps the noblest war of all, perhaps the only noble one. These wars caused considerable pain and suffering and thousands of bloody deaths.

But the deaths in all these wars, taken together, do not add up to the frightful number of deaths in just one war, the Civil War, where there were more killed than in all of our other wars combined.

251

Maybe it didn't have to happen; maybe it could have been avoided. Many people, and even serious historians, are always able to point the finger and place the blame on some incident or some event that was critical in bringing on the war, such as the "illegitimacy" (a word popular in January 2017) of Lincoln's election with only 39.8% of the popular vote; such as the reluctance of Southern landholders to free their slaves; such as the illegal secession of South Carolina from the Union; such as Lincoln's plans to invade the South to collect taxes; such as the unwarranted firing on Fort Sumter . . . Everything was someone else's fault: something else caused the war. Someone else was to blame.

So the different views crystalized and seemed irreconcilable; war was the only answer. Or was it? Lincoln thought so.

Many saw the war as hopelessly unavoidable. Some thought war would be all right so long as they were on the winning side. Some knew that war would be good for business. Some may even have tried to avoid war. President Buchanan was able to avoid war for four years by keeping cool and doing nothing, but it cost him the loss of respect and status in the eyes of many people and even historians in decades to come. If you think about it, you will note there is a high correlation between the popularity of our presidents and the number of people killed in war during their tenures of office. A prime example is Lincoln himself, our greatest president, and our greatest amount of killings. Other examples include Washington (the Revolution); Monroe (War of 1812); Jackson (Indian Wars); T. Roosevelt (Spanish-American War); Wilson

(World War One); F. Roosevelt (World War Two); Eisenhower (Korea); Kennedy and Johnson (Vietnam); Reagan and Bush (Middle East). Perhaps our only president who oversaw four years of no shooting and killing was Jimmy Carter, who therefore doesn't stand very high today in popularity in the eyes of most Americans. You gotta be a fighter if you wanna be popular. Many subsequent historians have rated James Buchanan the worse president we have ever had, the "do-nothing" president. All he did was keep us out of war for the four years he was president.

Virginia, North Carolina, Tennessee, and Arkansas were slave states that tried to maintain peace and avoid war by remaining in the Union after the Confederacy was formed, and even after Lincoln took office, to no avail. Lincoln lost the allegiance of these important states by his hasty decision to invade the South immediately after Fort Sumter, which Lincoln charged was a provocative insult to his presidential authority and therefore justification for the invasion plans he had already made. A big mistake. The four states strongly opposed an invasion, and felt they had to defend against it; accordingly they threw in their lot with their Southern brethren and joined the original seven states of the Confederacy. There were also important Republican politicians in various Northern states who favored "letting the South go," viewing it as a political liability and an economic millstone weighing heavily on the industrial prosperity of the North. Decades earlier, William Lloyd Garrison, recognizing that slavery was embedded in the US Constitution, seriously urged the secession of *New England* from the United States, as did many other Northerners going back to Thomas Pickering, George Cabot, and John Quincy Adams.

Some six weeks before the war began, and before Lincoln became president, a group of three notable representatives from Georgia, Alabama, and Louisiana went to Washington to see what they could do. Their names were Crawford, Forsythe, and Roman. They were known as "The Peace Commission." They had been given letters, papers, and documents from the fledgling Confederate Government delegating them with authority to consult and sign agreements on any and all matters of interest to the North and the South.

Although Lincoln was not yet president when the three-man "Commission" tried to present him with a letter from Jefferson Davis requesting an interview, he had to decline, apparently fearing that to receive these so-called emissaries would be tantamount to giving diplomatic recognition to the Southern Separatists and their so-called Confederacy. Why Lincoln believed this is unclear, for at the time, February 17, 1861, he was not yet president and held no official position with the Federal Government. One would think any such meeting could have been "off the record."

Dismayed and disappointed, but not completely disheartened or discouraged, Mr. Crawford and his cronies went on, pursuing their endeavors with Lincoln's favorite political associate, or *"eminence grise,"* William Seward, the man who was to become Lincoln's Secretary of State. Seward knew Lincoln's views and followed his path, and accordingly refused to meet with the little delegation just as Lincoln had refused. Unfortunately, neither Lincoln nor Seward knew anything about the details of what the Crawford Commission had to offer.

Jefferson Davis, a graduate of the United States Military Academy at West Point and a career Army officer, had had an illustrious military career, culminating in his heroic involvement in several important battles in the Mexican War. At first, Lt. Davis, and then Capt. Davis, fought valiantly although he was severely wounded. If he had died, we would have had monuments erected in his honor throughout the United States, but, alas, he lived on. A few years later he was made Secretary of War of the United States of America by President Franklin Pierce, and, as such, served with distinction throughout Pierce's term of office, from 1853 until 1857, almost to the eve of the Civil War. In his position as US Secretary of War, Davis completely renovated the Academy at West Point, making it the best military school in the world. Over a reluctant penny-pinching Congress, he was able to bring modern breech-loading guns, with rifled barrels, into the Army as the new standard weapon; these had far greater accuracy and reliability than the antiquated muzzle-loading muskets they replaced.

So when Davis was designated President of the Confederacy in February 1861 (he was never elected but was "designated" by the impromptu Southern legislature), he knew quite a bit about the strength of the Union Army, which he himself had done so much to build up and improve. He knew that, if the differences between the sections led to war, the South wouldn't have a chance. Besides out-numbering the South 2-to-1 or 3-to-1 in available manpower, the North had this fine, powerful army, which Davis himself had done so much to equip and strengthen. It is not hard to understand why Davis so strongly opposed the war. As United States Senator from

255

Mississippi, he spoke repeatedly of his concerns and his opposition to the looming War, on the floor of the Congress in 1860 and 1861.

Accordingly, the Crawford Peace Commission were given more than letters requesting interviews with President-elect Lincoln and other Union authorities. They were also given papers attesting to their authority to represent and speak for the Confederate States of America. And they were given even more, unwritten though much of it must have been. Davis, more than most of the leaders North or South, knew what horrors and devastation and death an all-out war would bring. Davis felt distressed, even desperate, with little more than Southern honor and fortitude confronting great Northern military power and efficiency. Davis told Crawford he must arrive at a peace agreement of some sort regardless of the conditions -- any conditions -- at any cost. Peace was the foremost thing, the only important thing, the *sine qua non* of a North-South agreement. War was out of the question.

* * * * *

Although Lincoln never knew it, nor did Seward or any other Northern authorities, Crawford had documents declaring that, if necessary to avoid war:

* The South will pay back taxes, which we hope
    will be reviewed for their propriety.

* The South will give up our slaves, which we
    hope will be carried out through a
    process of compensated emancipation.

256

* The South will pay any price the North may specify, to buy Fort Sumter (as South Carolina has already offered) and any other federal property still occupied on Confederate ground.

* The South will give unhesitating consideration to any other requests or demands of the North that may be necessary for, or conducive to, the avoidance of War.

* * * * *

Crawford's instructions from Davis and the Confederate Legislature, some of them simply verbal, went on to say that the only thing we ask for is the opportunity to save face before the body of our populace. Many Southerners, Davis said, are as stubborn and proud as were their Scots forebears. We do not so much mind doing what we know we have to do, but we, like the Scots, cannot stand to have it look as though we are doing merely what others have told us to do, even if to do so would be for our own good. Davis stressed that these considerations were necessary if the Confederate Government were to maintain authority and respect and control over its own people. So he told Crawford to try for an agreement that removed Federal tax-collectors from Southern soil. Let us pay voluntarily if that is the only way to avoid war. If we have to free our slaves to avoid war, at least let it appear to be our own decision and not one forced upon us. Just allow us to go on keeping the Negroes on our plantations and let us pay them a minimum wage. We would rather keep them as slaves, but will do anything to avoid war, even free them and pay them going wages.

257

Crawford may not have supported all of these things in his heart, but he was never put to the test, as neither Lincoln nor his minions would ever receive him or learn what he was authorized to say or offer.

So the war came, killing a total of over 600,000 soldiers, counting both sides, plus unknown numbers of collateral deaths of civilians, including women and children. Crawford ultimately died without ever having had the opportunity to reveal the extent of his peace-seeking authority. Lincoln also died, as we all know, also in ignorance of how he could have avoided the War. Davis survived post-war capture and imprisonment in chains for a time at Fort Monroe, finally dying in Mississippi in 1889. Of course, nobody lives forever. According to Wikipedia, "When General Basil W. Duke died in 1916, he was the oldest senior Confederate officer still alive."

All the others involved finally died too, but the chaos and devastation of the war, not to mention the racial hatreds it fomented, lingered on for decades to come. When Davis finally got to Heaven, he found Lincoln settled in a comfortable corner, having already been there almost twenty-five years.

"I'm sorry you got shot," said Davis to break the ice.

"Yeah, me too," said Lincoln. "But I must admit it did add quite a bit to my stature and my fame. You are always more famous if you can get yourself assassinated in the end."

"Nobody remembers me," said Davis, "although I did write an excellent book about all the good things I tried to do./1 Maybe you should have had *me* assassinated."

"I remember you," said Lincoln. "You're the one who started the war, aren't you?"

"Well yes, that's what they say. But in fact I tried to stop it before it began."

"You did? I didn't know that."

"Yes. Do you remember Martin Crawford? Crawford of Georgia? And John Forsythe of Alabama? And Andre Roman from Louisiana?"

"No, the names don't sound familiar. I don't think I ever knew any of those gentlemen."

"Yes, I know they never got to see you. They tried to meet with you on my behalf a week or two before you became president."

"They did? What for?"

"They were to negotiate with you. We authorized them to offer anything necessary to avoid that war, even to pay the taxes you wanted, or free our slaves and pay them wages. All we really wanted was to save face and have a little more say in our own affairs."

/1 *The Rise and Fall of the Confederate Government*, by Jefferson F. Davis.

"Really? I don't believe anyone told me about them. Maybe I should have listened to this Mr. Crawford and his friends."

"Yes, I think you should have."

THE ORIGINAL END

Epilogue

Although that's the end of the story, Lincoln took on a pensive mien and then asked, "Tell me, Jeff," he said, "if you had given up your Black slaves, do you think many of them would have come up to Illinois and the other Northern states?"

THE FINAL END

Bittersweet

I'm a pushover for a pretty woman, and a sucker for the tricks of the Devil. My early devilish memories go back to the time I was seven or eight years old and I let sweet Sally kiss me on the school bus./1   It got us in trouble, but I remember her very favorably nevertheless; indeed, I have always felt it was well worth it, all things considered.   I remember some other women too, from later years, some of them also favorably.   I cannot honestly say that I regret any of the times I fell in love.   I might have regretted the choice -- or the outcome, but probably not the fact of falling.

The truth is that I would have liked to be a rake, to be able to hop from one woman to another as circumstances and feelings waft to and fro over time, but alas I was not made that way. Over the years I did fall in love a few times -- once especially deeply and hopelessly.   Also, I was married twice, and naturally I loved both of my wives, at different times of course.   But after they had gone I fell in love with another woman that I was never married to. And a deep and special love it was. You see, I fell IN love with her without ever having LOVED her -- not in the modern sense, anyway.

Being in love is different from anything else in this world. (I don't know about Heaven yet.)   You can forget

---

/1 See THE YELLOW SCHOOL BUS in the first volume of the "Baked Alaska" series by Daniel Hoyt Daniels.

other things, but if you have ever been in love, really in love, you can never forget it, regardless of how far you got, or didn't get, with the young lady, or woman, or maiden, or whatever she was. And this special one I am thinking about retained her prominent position in my memory for many years.

Love can be bittersweet -- a two-edged sword, as Dumas and D'Artagnon would say. Sweet, certainly at the beginning, and sometimes even beyond that -- perhaps even for a lifetime for a lucky few, or so I've heard the poets say. Yes, it can be bitter, sad, and sometimes heartbreaking when it ends, or fades away, or, worst of all, when it is replaced.

I shall not bore anyone with giving the specifics of my falling in love with the particular woman I am thinking about -- one of the several women named Belinda I have known. Words not only fail to suffice to portray the emotional depth and beauty of the process, but also make the sublime look ridiculous, and the profound, trite. Poets have tried through the millennia to portray the essence of love, but few have succeeded in doing so, and I am not even a poet.

* * * * *

So there I was, only a few minutes after I first met this Belinda at my cousin Carol's supper party, already falling in love with her while I was still asking her what her name was. Fortunately I already knew a few Belindas, so that made it a bit easier to remember her name. Sometimes one Belinda would remind me of another. Sometimes, but not this time. This Belinda was different. She was beautiful and elegant, demure and gentle, knowledgeable and eloquent, attentive and graceful. And not even overweight. What else can I say? Bathed regularly? Table manners? Courtly posture? Graceful fingers? Lovely dinner dress with long shoulder straps? Oh my yes, all of these things.

But her eyes, and her voice, and the vibrations she radiated, penetrated me completely and captivated me from the first moment. (If you don't believe it is hard for me to write this down as I look back and think of these things, you would be mistaken.)

There is nothing so ridiculous and laughable as someone who is in love, or thinks he is in love, especially someone who is frustrated by an unrequited love. The only thing worse than an unrequited love is not knowing whether your love is requited or not -- not knowing whether she loves you back. You are afraid to blatantly ask her; you might in so doing clumsily extinguish some nascent little spark struggling to live. You try to tell yourself it is love indeed, and that, if it is true, it will survive. Love conquers all. That's what the poets say, isn't it? But what do they know about MY love? About me and Belinda? Nothing. I too know nothing. I have *feelings,* but I don't *know.*

I feel a lot of things: excitement, hope, passion, tenderness, concern, interest, camaraderie, bodily desire, attachment, and affection. And also that elusive L . . . word, with so many different meanings, hidden and unknown. What in God's name am I letting myself into?

* * * * *

Well, I guess the Devil knows. He probably arranged it all. Picked me up so he could drop me down.

That is a game the Devil likes to play. He will let you fall in love with a woman without revealing whether she loves you. Then before you have ever gotten anywhere with her, he breaks you up and lets you down -- breaks you apart. Then, for years, you are unable to fall in love with anyone else. Even though she is married to someone else by then, you think back and long to know whether she did once love you. You don't really expect ever to see her again, but you always hold some small, minuscule, hope nevertheless.

That's the way it was for a number of years. Then the Devil came to me one night at midnight when I was asleep and offered to cut a deal (sort of like he did with Eurydice and Orpheus, but I didn't know about them back then).

"I will tell you whether or not she once loved you, but if I do that, you must give up hope of ever seeing her again."

"How much chance do I have of ever seeing her again anyway?"

"Not very much," he said, "maybe one in a hundred."

Oh dear, what to do? I was aching to know whether she had ever had feelings of love for me, as I had had for her. But I would have been so overjoyed to see her again, even briefly, even now as an ugly old woman, that I hated to forgo that chance, however small it might be.

The Devil can be cruel.

Then Belinda unknowingly took matters into her own hands. Maybe she really did care a little. Maybe she was bored. Maybe she was just curious.

After a considerable period of no communication at all, in either direction, I got a short double-edged note from her, saying, "It's all right for you to write to me now. Klaus isn't jealous of you anymore."

My heart immediately leapt up as I beheld these words. I did not know Klaus at all, only that he was the one she took up with back then, soon after the last time I saw her. And Klaus didn't know anything about me, nothing more than Belinda herself might have told him. But jealous of me? How could he have been jealous of me? Answer: ONLY THROUGH WHAT BELINDA HERSELF MUST HAVE TOLD HIM. She must have told him, or strongly intimated along the way, that she had held some powerful tender feelings for me, or even LOVE! How else could he be jealous, not knowing anything more than that, about me or my acquaintance with his Belinda?

Oh joy! It can only mean she DID love me. She loved me! God be praised. I can sleep in peace now, until I die, in peace forever. My heart swelled, and a beatific euphoria spread through my body and my soul. For a while. That was the good news.

Then the bad news swept in right along behind. My thoughts continued to swirl about and bubble up and down. Oh, if only I could have stopped thinking at that moment, how sweet life would have been. But my thoughts rambled on, out of control.

"*Not jealous anymore.*" Not *now* jealous. It must mean she is telling him that he doesn't have anything now to be jealous about. I shut my eyes, and I could hear her telling him, with penetrating tones of unwonted honesty, "Oh, Klaus, my Darling, maybe I did think I loved him a smidgen a long time ago, and that might have upset you, but it was really nothing. Besides, that was before you came into my life and showed me the real thing. You are the only one I have ever loved, and I certainly don't love that fellow -- never really did. Now, let's end this and turn out the light and go to sleep. Good night, my Love."

My eyes filled with tears. My heart deflated. My excitement expired. My essence perished. I too felt like expiring. But now I knew everything I had wanted to know: I had confirmed and justified my misery and sorrow. It was over, as I had, deep down, known all along, against all hope. I had known it was over; I had only wanted proof. Closure. Burial.

The Devil had played out his little game. I no longer had to wonder. Yes, apparently there might have once been some love, at least a spark, a tiny spark, but no more. The spark was out. Nothing left but a persistent and fleeting memory of hopeless hope. Tiny ash of a burned-out Lucifer match.

THE END

Epilogue.

E-mail from Maria Blois, March 9, 2018

Oh my goodness. This is so beautiful. I love it so much. I love the title bittersweet. You are such an amazing incredible man! This story has touched me so. I have tears in my eyes. I will always treasure it.

To see someone love my mother the way she deserves to be loved. To see her through your eyes. Beautiful. Just breathtakingly beautiful. What a gift. Thank you, precious Uncle Dan, for sharing this with me. I love you. Maria.

THE FINAL END

Other works by Daniel Hoyt Daniels

VERSE TRANSLATIONS OF MOLIÈRE COMEDIES:
Volume One: DON JUAN AND OTHER PLAYS
  "The Imaginary Cuckold"
  "A Doctor in Spite of Himself"
  "Don Juan"
Volume Two: THE MISANTHROPE AND OTHER PLAYS
  "Love is the Best Doctor"
  "A School for Husbands"
  "The Misanthrope"
Volume Three: THE IMAGINARY INVALID AND OTHER PLAYS
  "George Dandin"
  "The Learnèd Ladies"
  "The Imaginary Invalid"

"BAKED ALASKA and Other SHORT SHORT STORIES"
BAKED ALASKA
HEADS I WIN, TAILS I WIN
STORMY NIGHT
GOOD NEWS
THE LIVE OAK
THE RABBIT
BITCHES ON THE BEACH
HELLO THERE
PLAYING IT COOL
MAKING ARRANGEMENTS
THAT'S OKAY
ANYTHING YOU WANT
GETTING EVEN
HASTA LA VISTA
IT WOULDN'T BE ADVISABLE
A NEW START
THE PRODIGAL CALF
A FEW MORE DAYS
LIKE I SAID, AN ORDINARY GUY
TURKEY IN THE STRAW
JOHN HARVARD FANTOMA
MY BROTHER-IN-LAW IS A JERK
THE MOUSTACHE
MONEY, MONEY, MONEY
THE WORLD OF ART
THE BEARD
BASTILLE DAY – PROVING A POINT
LOCKS OF GOLD
HYPOCRISY, ANYONE ?
YOU TOOK THE WORDS

Other works by Daniel Hoyt Daniels

"THIRTY OF THE BEST SHORT STORIES"

A SCOUNDREL, MY FATHER
SORRY, I'M BUSY
THUMBS UP
THE FAITHFUL WIFE
OH, DIDN'T YOU KNOW?
THE TELEGRAM
THE LAST WORD
DIVORCE OLD FRENCH STYLE
WHITE MAN IN A BLACK SKIN
A HALLOWE'EN GHOST STORY
TOOTHPASTE, ANYONE?
WITHOUT MY GLASSES
RUN, RUN !
THE SECRET
I DIDN'T KNOW
COLLEGE TUITION
THE GRUDGE
HORSES
I WASN'T QUITE ABLE
IT'S YOUR COW
THE DOUBLE AGENT
HAPPY THANKSGIVING
REWRITING HISTORY
HOLY COW
00THE BEST OF TIMES
DO YOU THINK YOU CAN?
WHAT'S IN A NAME
UNCLE CHARLIE
PRETTY GOOD ENGLISH
THE ASTROLOGER AND THE KING

Other works by Daniel Hoyt Daniels

"SHORT STORIES GALORE"

PENNIES FROM HEAVEN
ONCE A BUTLER
THE ABUSED CHILD
KEEPING IT LEGAL
WAITING AWAY
A PROPER UPBRINGING
ALTRUISM -- LOVE OF LIFE
AFFAIR, ANYONE ?
THE DREAM
ALWAYS IN LOVE
YOU'LL LOVE IT
CHINESE CHESS
THE DIPLOMATIC WEIGHT-WATCHER
TENOR, ANYONE ?
AND SO HE DID
THE MILLIONAIRE
HARMONY
MÉNAGE À TROIS
DISAPPOINTMENT
THANKS FOR THE MEMORY
BEST FOOT FORWARD
ONCE A KING, or THE RIVALRY
OLDER WOMAN
DOUBLE TAKE
MOTHER TONGUE
COUNT YOUR BLESSINGS
THE SIXTY-SECOND WORKOUT
DON'T LET IT BOTHER YOU
I ASSURE YOU
THE BRAIN

Other works by Daniel Hoyt Daniels

"SHORT STORIES FOREVER"

BEFORE HE EVER DIED
THE ORACLE
THE YELLOW SCHOOL BUS
MAD
SORRY, NO SPANISH
THE PROMISE
ECUMENICAL
MY SISTER'S BUTLER
YES SIR, OFFICER!
THE DEBUTANTE
STORY TELLING
IF YOU SHOOT IT
I COULDN'T AFFORD IT
GETTING WARMER
REPENTANCE
NIKE
HOW DEGRADING
OH, ALL RIGHT
DOLORES
RETIRED
I'LL SHOW YOU!
WHERE DID WE COME FROM?
USE YOUR PHONE
ONE GOOD ONE
DISTANT RELATIVE
THE WINDOW
THE BALLAD OF GOOD NEWS
FRIENDSHIP
HAPPY FELLA
PAIRING THE VOTE

Other works by Daniel Hoyt Daniels

"SHORT STORIES ENCORE"

VIRUS INFECTION
HITTING FOR THE CIRCUIT
WRONG ANSWER
CONNECTING
THE PREDICTION
RAINY DAY
POINT OF VIEW
THE ROBBERY
THE BEAUTY OF THIS WORLD
WHAT DO YOU SAY?
OPENING DAY
TRUE LOVE
MY SUGGESTION IS
NOVEL MATERIAL
KILL OR BE KILLED
BELIEVING
OH, WOE IS ME
FIFTY CENTS
GAME COCKS
REMEMBERING GUERNICA
CONVERSION
GOOD LUCK
CONSUMMATION
JUSTIFIABLE
A FRIEND IN NEED
LIBERTY OR DEATH
TELL IT TO THE JUDGE
ALWAYS TRUE
A CIVIL WAR STORY
THE CERTIFICATE

Other works by Daniel Hoyt Daniels

"GRAMMAR TODAY"
Comprising a few more Rules Ruge (Ferdinand E.Ruge) would have espoused for proper English usage

ABBREVIATIONS
ADJECTIVE USED AS ADVERB
AGREEMENT OF SUBJECT AND VERB
ALRIGHT -- ALL RIGHT
APPRAISE -- APPRISE
COLLECTIVE NOUNS
COMMAS ON PARENTHETICAL EXPRESSIONS
COMPARISON OF ADJECTIVES
COMPRISE -- CONSTITUTE
DANGLING PARTICIPLES AND GERUNDS
DEFINITE -- DEFINITIVE
EACH OTHER -- ONE ANOTHER
   BETWEEN -- AMONG
EXPECTATIONS -- GOALS AND OBJECTIVES
FALSE ELLIPSIS
FIGURATIVE SENSE
FORBID -- FORBADE
FURTHER -- FARTHER
GERUNDS -- USE OF THE POSSESSIVE WITH GERUNDS
HEALTHY -- HEALTHFUL
I -- ME
"IF" CLAUSES, SUBJUNCTIVE OR NOMINATIVE?
IMPACT -- AFFECT
IMPACT -- EFFECT
INCREDIBLE -- UNBELIEVABLE
INCREDULOUS -- INCREDIBLE
IN EXCESS OF
LAPSES OF LOGIC, AND STUPIDITIES
LESS -- FEWER
"LET'S" MEANS "LET US"
LIE AND LAY -- SIT AND SET
LIKE
LIKE -- AS IF, AS THOUGH
MYSELF -- ME, I
NOT HELP BUT
ONE OF THOSE WHO
OVERWORKED PREPOSITION
PARTICIPLES ENDING WITH -ING
PAST PERFECT TENSE -- PAST TENSE
PLUS -- FURTHERMORE
PREPOSITION ASSOCIATED WITH VERB -- LOSS OF
SOMEPLACE -- PLACE
SPECIAL PLURALS
SUBJUNCTIVE FALLING INTO DISUSE
THAT -- VERY
TRANSITIVE VERB REQUIRES OBJECT
TWO SUBORDINATE CLAUSES
UNCOUNTABLE NOUNS
UNDER -- LESS THAN
VERB OR NOUN? -- PRONUNCIATION
WARMER TEMPERATURES -- HIGHER TEMPERATURES
WHICH -- THAT
WHO -- WHOM
WITH REGARDS TO
WOULD -- WOULD

273

Other works by Daniel Hoyt Daniels

"SHORT STORIES YOU'LL LOVE"

BREAKFAST AT TIFFANY'S
THE PIECE OF GOLD
GOT RELIGION?
COMPLETE COVERAGE
THE RANSOM
MALICE TOWARD NONE
SWITCH HITTER
GENEALOGY BEWARE
JEANETTE LOVES RICHARD
DEPRESSION DANDELIONS
LITTLE MONKEYS
JOHNNY O'TOOLE
EAU DE COLOGNE
LIKE FATHER LIKE SON
I 'M SO SORRY
THE BRIDGE
MOST ENJOYMENT
TRUE VALUE
THE EMBEZZLER
THE DANCER
THE TRAITOR
GOD HELP ME
FOR SERVICES RENDERED
ENEMY'S ENEMY
CAT AND MOUSE
DOUBLE JEOPARDY
WHO AM I ?
THE OLD ACTOR
GOOD COOK, TOUGH DECISION
A BETTER WAY

CPSIA information can be obtained
at www.ICGtesting.com
Printed in the USA
FFHW02n0008131018
48802668-52953FF